SECOND CHANCE AT US

A SMALL TOWN BILLIONAIRE ROMANCE

EMMA REESE

INTRODUCTION

I'm a billionaire rockstar taking a break in my sleepy
hometown.
She's my sister's newly-single best friend.

I can't stop staring at her.
But I need to focus.
This is my first solo gig without the band.

The way she bites her lip...
The way that outfit hugs her every curve perfectly...
The way our eyes lock, as if time itself stands still.

Now we're alone in my dressing room.
Inches apart.
The air is electric with unspoken desire.
With every breath, I can almost taste her.

I can't take it anymore.
I need her up against that wall.

But her barriers are up.
I'm running out of time.

Can I finally explain why I left her at that concert years ago?
This time, I won't let our song remain unfinished.

1

DARCY

"**O**h, my God! Look who it is!"

The shrieking from the other side of the room drew my attention. What was going on over there? I was hosting an open house, which was going great. The home buzzed with potential buyers, and I was starting to think we might even secure an offer before the end of the day! But then all those potential clients started rushing out of the kitchen, heading back to the front door.

"What's going on?" I asked Liz, my best friend and partner in our real estate firm.

"No idea," Liz shrugged. "Maybe check it out?"

Liz popped another cookie into her mouth and returned to inputting email addresses into our database. Clearly, she wasn't concerned. We positioned ourselves at the kitchen island, ready to answer questions as people milled about the house. The kitchen was open to the living room, but we couldn't see the front door from where we stood.

"Fine, but if you hear me scream, come get me," I laughed.

I left my clipboard on the counter and crossed to the

entryway. I had worn heels, something I rarely did, and I heard them click across the beautiful hardwood floors of the house. Hardwood floors and bay windows were the details that filled my life these days. With a few more sales, Liz and I could buy another office building in the neighboring town. We were looking for ways to expand our reach.

"*Pleeease,* can I have a picture?"

The commotion from the other room was only getting louder. I tucked my blonde hair behind my ear—a nervous habit. I had no idea what I might find, and I was hesitant to find out.

"Alright, ladies. Let's take it easy."

The voice stopped me in my tracks.

Is that ...? But, no, it couldn't be—the last I knew he was somewhere in Singapore. Surely Liz would have told me if he was back in town?

As I crossed into the entryway, a few women looked back at me. A redhead directly in front of me even stepped aside, looking a bit embarrassed to be caught trying to get the man's autograph. And there, standing half a head taller than the women around him, his dark, curly hair covering his eyes in a way that looked accidental but was perfectly intentional, was Callum Jones.

I gasped when I saw him, horrified to see that this drew his attention toward me. His eyes caught mine, and there was a spark of recognition. Was that a smile? I felt my face flush hot, and I instantly turned around. I almost tripped as I rushed as fast as I could back to the kitchen.

"Liz!" I hissed, trying not to make a scene in front of the guests who *hadn't* ambushed Callum Jones at our open house.

"What?" Liz asked, avoiding eye contact. She was far too relaxed, as if she were feigning innocence.

"What is your *brother* doing at our open house?"

"Is he here?" Liz asked, but she could barely get the words out before breaking into a smile. "I'm sorry I didn't tell you!"

"You didn't think you should let me know your rock-star brother was planning to walk through the front door of our open house today?"

"Actually, I told him to pick the back door. He never listens to me."

"*Liz!*"

"Alright, I'm sorry. I knew you would be upset. But he wanted to say hello to you."

"He's here to see *me?*"

Liz didn't respond right away. Instead, she began rearranging the cookies on the plate in front of her, as if it were a crucial task for the success of the open house.

"I thought you might be excited," Liz shrugged, avoiding my gaze.

"Excited?" I cried out, a bit too loud. One of the guests exploring the living room looked over at me with concern but quickly looked away. I needed to calm down. I took a deep breath and tried to bring my mind back to the room and the job in front of me.

You're a professional realtor, I reminded myself. *Don't let some jerk from your past ruin everything in front of you.*

This was a mantra I had been repeating a lot lately. After breaking up with my fiancé six months ago, I had committed to work and myself. I didn't have time for men to complicate things when there was so much to accomplish in front of me. And this commitment to my job and our business was actually working. The past three months had been filled with positive steps forward for Dream Home Realty, with unprecedented business growth. No way could I let a surprise visit from Callum Jones destroy everything I had worked so hard for.

"I know you had a falling out in high school," Liz said, turning to look me in the eye for the first time since Callum's appearance. "But that was a long time ago. Maybe it's time to start fresh."

"He totally embarrassed me, Liz," I said, nearly whispering. "I was just some joke he could laugh about with his friends."

"He's a different person now," Liz said. "Maybe you can give him a second chance?"

I saw the hopeful expression on my friend's face. Liz's love for her brother and her allegiance to me as her best friend tore her apart. We were two of the most important people in Liz's life, and I knew she wanted us to get along. Or, at least, tolerate being in the same room together. I also knew that, on some level, holding on to this grudge for so many years was a bit irrational. But every time I saw Callum's face pop up in the media, I felt a wash of shame as I thought about our one and only date all those years ago.

"Can you just give it a try for me?" Liz asked.

I sighed, unable to say no to someone I had been best friends with since the fourth grade.

"I promise not to be openly hostile," I said, smirking at Liz to show that I was joking. Well, sort of. "How long is he here for?"

"All summer," Liz said, and my eyebrows shot up in surprise as my mouth fell open in shock. *All summer?* I expected Liz to say a few days, maybe a week. I didn't think I would have to play nice for *months.*

My mind flew to all the times I might run into Callum in this small town. I pictured him at my favorite cafe, ordering a coffee as he smiled at the girls behind the counter. I imagined him popping into our real estate office, maybe dropping off Liz's children after a day at the playground. There would be no way to avoid him. I inwardly groaned. This was going to be a difficult summer ...

"Doesn't he have a tour to get back to?"

"He's taking a break," Liz explained. "It's been a lot for him. Traveling to different cities every night, jumping from country to country. He hasn't slept in his own bed for almost a year! And you know he hasn't visited for ages. The kids hardly remember they *have* an uncle. So I convinced him to take some time off."

Callum was a singer and guitar player for a huge rock band, the Horizon. They formed the first year Callum was at college and quickly shot to fame, releasing their first album when he was barely twenty. Three albums later, and the group was selling out stadiums and making appearances on late-night talk shows. As the lead singer and primary songwriter, Callum was the face of the band, which meant wherever he went, fans recognized him.

"I think he needs the time away," Liz said, worry causing a crease between her eyebrows. "He's been so tired lately. And his manager's putting so much pressure on him to get his face out there. Sounds like all his manager talks about is 'momentum' and 'riding the wave of fame'. Hopefully, some time at home can let him relax a little bit."

I thought back to Callum bombarded by fans in the entryway. He was still there, signing autographs and taking pictures. Did he look tired when I saw him? When I saw pictures of him, I always took the messy hair and circles under Callum's eyes as a calculated rock-star look. But I had to admit there were aspects of Callum's life I would never want to experience first-hand.

"Hopefully," I said, agreeing with Liz. "Though he can't

even attend a small-town open house without people wanting his attention. I'm not sure he'll get too much relief."

"True," Liz said, closing her computer and standing up. "But the town's so small that *eventually* everyone will have their autograph and we can all move on. I better go save him."

Liz walked away toward the entryway, heading off to rescue her older brother. Like Callum, Liz had dark, curly hair. She often wore hers pulled back in a ponytail. Where Callum was tall and broad, Liz was petite, barely coming up to her brother's shoulder. I had always been slightly taller than average, and everyone liked to make fun of the height difference between us as we went through middle school and high school.

As Liz walked away, I made the rounds in the living room, forcing myself back to my work. I checked in with the people opening closet doors and discussing the level of sunlight coming through the windows. But even as I smiled and handed out my business card, I couldn't ignore Callum only a room away from me. What was it about him that made me nervous and excited all at once?

I thought back to the moment our eyes met in the entryway. There had been such a warmth on Callum's face. If I didn't know any better, I would say he was excited to see me. And then there were Liz's words floating through my head: *He wanted to say hello to you.* The man was a billionaire rock star. He had his pick of women wherever he went. But Liz said he wanted to see *me*?

I shook my head to clear these thoughts, reminding myself of the job at hand. The only focus should be on selling this house. Crossing back to the fridge, I pulled out a few more water bottles and carefully placed them on the counter. Tidying up the stack of flyers that gave important details on the house and even rearranged the curtains hanging over the sink's window. Anything to keep my hands and mind occupied.

But just as I turned back to check on the platter of cookies on the kitchen island, I caught sight of Liz walking into the living room. And right behind her, looking tall and handsome as ever, was Callum. I watched his eyes quickly scan the room in front of him before sweeping over to the kitchen. Once again, our eyes locked, and I couldn't ignore the way the side of his mouth curved up, a smirk of excitement and recognition that took my breath away.

Panic coursed through my veins as I watched Callum and Liz get closer, clearly headed right toward me. What would I say when he was here? What would *he* say? All at once, I felt like a teenage girl, tongue-tied and nervous around my crush. What if I made a fool of myself? Or what if he tried to bring up that horrible date we had all those years ago?

An older woman who had been pointing out the living room's skylight to her husband suddenly caught sight of Callum as he passed. She grabbed his arm, and it was enough to pull Callum's attention away from me. He looked over at the woman, and I watched him plaster a fake smile onto his face, ready to greet an adoring fan.

This was my chance. Before I could think about what I was doing, I grabbed my purse and bolted toward the side door of the house that was off of the kitchen. I caught Liz's eye and mouthed "I'm sorry," as my hand found the door handle.

And then, I ran away from my own open house.

2

CALLUM

"My husband just loves you. Don't you, Oliver?"

I forced a smile as the woman who had just grabbed my arm pushed her husband in front of me. I tried to feign interest in the couple, even as my eyes scanned the room behind them, searching. The husband, Oliver, was spouting on about his favorite song on our most recent album, and I tried to nod enough to convince the man I was paying attention. But my real interest was in someone else. Where was Darcy?

I went to the open house hoping I would run into Darcy Stevens. After all, she ran a business with my sister, Liz. Every time Liz mentioned Darcy's name on our frequent phone calls, I felt a flash of excitement as I thought about her. It was strange, considering I hadn't seen her for over ten years. Even more surprising was how my breath caught in my throat when I saw Darcy for the first time after all those years. Or the way my heart pounded when we locked eyes.

Now I struggled to look around Oliver's balding head to catch Darcy's gaze once more.

"It was a group effort," I said, using some of my stock

responses when I spoke about the Horizon's most recent album. "Everyone contributes a little bit to make these things successful."

There! I caught sight of Darcy over the man's shoulder, but she wasn't looking at me. Instead, she grabbed her purse and headed to the door. Wait! Where was she going?

"Would you excuse me?" I asked, interrupting the couple who were now telling me all about their grandchildren. I pushed past them, an uncharacteristic move for me, and I heard Liz apologizing on my behalf. But I was only focused on one thing: I had to talk to Darcy.

But just as I pushed my way around the couple, I saw Darcy slipping out through the side door, a hard slam drawing the attention of a few people standing around us. I felt the energy drain out of me as I realized Darcy had disappeared.

"Sorry, man," Liz said, appearing next to me. "I think she's a little spooked."

"Spooked? What did you say to her?"

My sister tended to meddle a bit too much in my business. I couldn't help wondering what Liz had said to Darcy to freak her out.

"Nothing!" Liz said, putting her hands up in the air like someone about to be arrested. "I just said you were looking forward to saying hello."

"Why did you do that? No wonder she's freaked out."

"I thought it would make things better! Let the two of you have a fresh start."

"Fresh start? We hardly know each other."

"Not anymore. But there was that date …" Liz let her voice trail off, letting me know there was something more she wanted to say.

"When we were teenagers?" I thought back to that time.

I remembered my friend group hanging out with Darcy and hers here and there. That was in the last summer before I went to college. For a little while I thought Darcy might be interested in me, but that first and only date told me definitively that she wasn't.

"That was a million years ago," I said. "We were just kids then. Times have changed.

But even as I said this to Liz, I wasn't sure I believed it. If Darcy didn't like me back then, what made me think she would like me now? Maybe I should take Darcy fleeing the house for what it looked like: she wanted nothing to do with me.

"Cheer up," Liz said, jabbing her elbow into my arm. "It's a long summer. You have lots of time to meet someone."

A man came to ask Liz a question about the layout of the second floor, and she walked away, heading toward the stairs. I was left standing alone at the kitchen island, wondering why I had bothered to come here. Even after all these years of fame and attention, perhaps because of it, I still felt bad in the face of rejection. Rejection from someone I actually liked was particularly difficult for me. Someone I wanted to get to know better.

I was looking for something *real* in my life. Not the endless string of women who hung around me on tour, more attracted to fame than the guy underneath it. Some part of me had fantasized about finding someone in my hometown who might see me for *me* rather than the character I played. I realized now how stupid that idea was.

I felt my phone buzz in my pocket and pulled it out and saw my manager's name pop up on the screen. This made me groan. The last person I wanted to talk to was my fast-talking, money-obsessed manager. But I knew the man well enough to know he would keep calling until I picked up. And he would only get more animated and upset the longer it took me to answer.

I slipped outside through the same door Darcy had left by and picked up the phone.

"Hey Brady," I said, trying to keep the annoyance out of my voice.

"Callum! My man! Where are you?"

"At my sister's real estate open house," I said. "Didn't you get my email?"

"I did, buddy, I did. It's why I'm calling. Look, I knew you were heading home for a charity concert. That's all good, man. But this email says you're going home for the *summer*. The band itinerary has you home for three nights. We can't lose you for three *months*, man."

I sighed as I heard Brady's words, even though I wasn't surprised to hear them. I knew Brady wouldn't be happy about my email announcement telling him I was taking three months off. I knew it was the cowardly way to communicate, but if I'd tried to talk to Brady in person, I would still be in Singapore. Lately, it felt like I was constantly on a different page to Brady and the rest of my band.

"I know, Brady," I said, running my hand through my hair. "But we've been going nonstop. Don't you think we could all use some time off?"

"But our momentum, man!" It was Brady's favorite thing to talk about: Momentum. Keeping things *hot*. Staying on top of fame. They were Brady's constant refrains.

I held the phone away from my ear as Brady started pontificating on what hard work it took to be a rock star.

"Like you would know," I muttered under my breath. Luckily, Brady was too in love with the sound of his own voice to hear my dig. As Brady prattled on, I felt anger and frustration rising in my body. I knew I needed to move, or I might explode, so I started walking. The house Liz and Darcy had been showing wasn't far from the town's Main Street, and I took off toward it, excited to see all the old haunts of my childhood.

"You don't know what you've got until it's gone," Brady told me through the phone, as if this were some nugget of information I should find brilliant. Brady was constantly stealing people's lines and making them his own.

"Doesn't absence make the heart grow fonder?" I asked, smirking to myself. I couldn't help messing with Brady a bit, throwing famous lines and sayings right back at him.

"That might be true for your love life, but not for rock and roll," Brady told me. He launched off into a list of the theaters and arenas that were ready to book our band for a summer tour. It didn't surprise me that Brady was pushing us to keep performing. After all, Brady got a big cut of any money the band made. And despite the hundreds of thousands of dollars my bandmates and I had raked in for Brady, it never seemed to be enough for the guy.

"Brady, look," I said, ready to put an end to this conversation. "I'm taking the summer off. You can't convince me otherwise. And I already cleared it with the guys."

"The other guys are ready to go back out," Brady assured me. "They're ready to extend the tour."

I sighed again as I passed a cafe I didn't recognize. The decor was bright and rustic, making the place look more like the hipster coffee shops I usually saw in major cities. When did Maplewood get something so modern?

"They're at a different place in their lives, Brady," I said. I glanced at the posters hanging up in the windows of the cafe, advertising community theater musicals and the local farmer's market. As my eyes crossed from poster to poster, I was surprised to see my own face staring back at me: *Callum Jones. One Night Only. A special acoustic event.*

This concert was how I convinced Brady to let me come home.

"I got a solo gig back home in Maplewood," I had told him. "It's a fundraising event. Something to give back to the community. I'll be home for a few days, tops."

Brady had loved the idea—he wouldn't stop talking about the "positive public relations angle". He pitched the story of a benefit concert in my hometown to reporters and radio personalities all over the country to drum up positive press.

It was only my email this morning that told Brady this little trip home would be for a more extended period.

"You know I've been eager to try things on my own," I said, letting frustration filter into my voice. I was trying not to yell at Brady, but I needed my manager to listen to me. "I *told* you I want to work on a solo album. I've wanted that for a long time."

"But it's not the *right* time—" Brady started, but I cut him off.

"Enough, Brady!" I yelled. "You're not listening to me. I've been trying to tell you for *months* that I need a break. I've been telling you I'm unhappy running around from city to city and taking red eyes to God knows where. And you haven't listened. So I'm taking the summer off. And you all need to deal with it."

I hung up with a grunt and had the urge to throw my phone onto the pavement. Luckily, I kept my cool and simply shoved my phone into my back pocket with enough energy it tested the seams. I took off down the street, walking with all the anger that had accumulated in my body.

I was tired of people not listening to me. Brady was high on this list, but my bandmates were also to blame. For months I had been trying to tell them I was burned out. The pressure of writing all our music and serving as the lead singer and guitar player in the band was weighing on me, especially with a full tour schedule. But no one seemed to hear me. They simply asked about new music and then talked about what they were having for dinner.

And so, when Liz invited me for the summer, laying on a lot of guilt about how I was going to forget what my niece and nephew looked like, I said yes. It was the break I needed. Brady calling me today had just solidified how much I needed this time away to decide what I really wanted.

Telling Brady off made me feel a little better. Letting the adrenaline of that conversation rush out of me, I walked down Main Street and even smiled as I passed the comic book shop I used to visit as a kid. Having not been back to town since college, it was fun to recognize the stores, trees, and road signs from my past.

As I passed a new clothing store, I recognized the hardware store on the corner that had been in town long before I was born. I remembered visiting the place as a kid. But from my spot across the street I could see the shades drawn, and a "Closed" sign in the window. It was strange the store was closed on a Saturday.

Just as I was about to keep walking, another sign caught my eye in the window, this one nearly as surprising as seeing my own face on that poster: "For Sale".

The hardware store's for sale? I thought. It was the last

place I would expect to shut down. I had an unmistakable urge to see inside again, to remember visiting with my grandfather and helping him pick out the right-size screws for whatever project he was working on in the garage.

I crossed the street to get a better look.

3

DARCY

"I feel lost, Dad."

I stood in the middle of my dad's hardware store, talking to the empty room.

The smell of sawdust and leather wafted around me, bringing back memories of running through the store's aisles as a kid. I had spent many happy afternoons after school refilling buckets of screws and sorting the bolts by size as my dad rang people up on the cash register that was almost as old as the building.

This hardware store had been in our family since 1901 when my great-great-great-grandfather opened its doors to the town. Generations of my family had run the store, helping neighbors pick out shovels for their gardens or telling them what paintbrush to buy. As I stood in the aisles, I could picture all the families who had been in and out of our front door.

It's what made me so sad the place was currently closed.

My dad passed away eight months ago from an aggressive cancer that moved far too quickly. Not that any amount of time with my dad would have been enough. After my mom died when I was young, my dad was a single parent, seeing me through all the usual childhood milestones all by himself. He had coached my soccer team and learned how to braid my hair for school picture days.

And our relationship had only grown closer as I grew up. As an adult, I spent a few nights a week at my dad's house, either cooking dinner for him or showing up with takeout. Losing my dad was something I was still reeling from. It had been so unexpected. And then there was the breakup ...

I realized a few months ago that losing my dad had also been the beginning of the end for my engagement to John. After my dad died, I realized that life was too short to spend time with people I didn't truly love.

"What if there's nothing here for me anymore?"

Sometimes, when I felt especially confused, I found myself talking out loud in this old building. It wasn't like I believed in ghosts or expected my dad to talk back or anything. But this hardware store had always been my safe space. If I was going to voice my deepest and darkest secrets, there was no better place than these aisles of household goods.

Sometimes, when I thought about losing my dad and ending my engagement all in the span of a year, I wondered why I still lived in Maplewood. I had Liz and my business. Both of those things were going great. But there wasn't much else here for me. Sometimes I couldn't help but wonder if there was something else I was supposed to find out there.

My phone buzzed in my purse, and I fished it out to see that Liz was calling me. No doubt she would ask why I'd bailed on the open house. I could only hope things hadn't gotten too crazy, and that Liz had managed on her own.

"I know," I said as I picked up the phone. "I'm sorry I left."

"We got an offer!" Liz cried out, not even listening to my apology. "*Three* offers, actually. But one of them is *really* promising."

"*How* promising?" I asked, catching on to Liz's excitement through the phone.

"How's ten thousand over asking for you?"

Liz and I screamed into the phone, and I bounced with excitement.

"That's amazing," I said. "I'm telling you, you really are the best closer in the business."

"I think it's time we put it on my business cards."

"Maybe a plaque?"

"And definitely my own parking space."

I laughed with Liz, relishing the high that came from doing our jobs well and reaping the benefits.

"But seriously, Liz, I'm sorry I bailed. I shouldn't have done that."

"First you and then Callum. Good thing I'm pretty good at handling crowds. It got busy there today!"

"Callum ditched you too?"

"Right after you left," Liz explained. "I think he got a phone call, and he's always been a walker. He can't stay still, you know. Where he ended up is anyone's guess."

"You lost your rock-star brother on his first day in town?"

"It sounds bad when you say it like that," Liz laughed.

"Just don't let the tabloids find out."

"He'll turn up," Liz assured me. "They always come back when they're hungry."

There was a brief silence on the line, and then Liz asked, "Are you okay?"

I sighed, realizing I had been asking myself that very question only a few minutes ago.

"I'm fine," I tried to assure her. "I don't know why I got so freaked out when Callum showed up. It was just … unexpected."

"I should have told you he was coming. I really misjudged that one."

"A little bit," I chuckled.

"I thought you might be excited."

"Do you know me at all?" I asked, though there was a lightness to my voice that told Liz I was joking. "I'm not really someone who likes surprises. You know I need time to think through all the possible scenarios for what might go wrong!"

"I don't know if even *you* could have predicted running out of the house before even speaking to him."

I groaned, realizing how ridiculous it must have looked.

"Did I completely embarrass myself?" I asked.

"Don't worry about it—he was distracted by this older couple who wanted to show him pictures of their grandchildren. Where did you go, anyway? I'm heading back to the office now."

"I'm not there," I said. "I stopped by the hardware store."

"Oh," Liz said, and in her voice, I heard a question. "You didn't get an offer, did you?"

"No," I said. "No new offers. I just needed a spot to think."

A few months ago, I had put my dad's store on the market. After all, my dad and I both knew I was never going to be passionate about the hardware store business. Despite working in the store through high school, I couldn't drum up excitement for garden rakes and mousetraps. But instead of being disappointed, my dad had been nothing but excited for me.

"You get to go out there and find the thing you love," he would tell me often.

It felt good to have his blessing to move into a different profession. And my dad had been so proud when I got my real estate license and opened my office. But that didn't mean I found it any easier to walk away from my family's business and legacy.

"Have you had any showings lately?" Liz asked. "There have to be people interested in that place—it's one of the best retail spots in town!"

"There's interest," I said, but I let my voice trail off, leaving something unspoken. Of course, Liz caught onto it immediately.

"Not the *right* interest?"

"I don't know," I sighed, walking to the checkout counter to drop onto the stool. "I know I'm dragging my feet on it. And I know my dad would want me to let the place go. But it feels wrong to sell the place to someone who's going to gut it and put in an ice cream shop."

"*Ooh,* we could totally use a good frozen-yogurt place!"

"*Liz!*" I cried out, laughing along with Liz on the other end of the phone.

"I know you don't want to hear it," Liz said, her voice much more serious. "But you might be looking for a unicorn. In a small town like Maplewood, I'm not sure you're going to find someone who wants to buy a building just to keep it running as a hardware store."

"I know."

"It's not like your dad was raking in the money. These old, town hardware stores are sort of a dying breed these days."

I hated to admit that Liz might be right. The idea that someone would come along to buy the store and keep it exactly the same was probably a fantasy. But if I was going to let the store out of my family, I at least wanted to find a buyer who would preserve some part of the store's legacy. Was it so hard to imagine someone who might pick up right where my dad left off?

"I'm willing to wait," I told Liz. "I still have hope the right person is out there."

To Liz's credit, she had never pushed me when it came to the hardware store. Despite the store's listing with our office and the potential commission we were set to receive if the building was sold, Liz knew this building was my own thing. And so far, she seemed prepared to let me deal with the building in my own time.

"It's alright," Liz said. "Take the time you need."

"Thanks," I said.

I glanced down at the desk where mail had piled up on the counter. Pulling the stack to me, I flipped through the envelopes I had been avoiding. I knew I would find bills and invoices in most of them. Settling my dad's estate and planning a funeral had all come with endless expenses I hadn't anticipated. And then there were all the canceled wedding expenses: a lost deposit on the venue, an invoice from the graphic designer who made the invites, a bill from the seamstress. Selling this building could go a long way toward paying off these debts.

"I'm at the office," Liz said, pulling me out of my thoughts. "I'll drop everything off, and then I have to pick up the kids from camp. Do you need anything else today?"

"You closed another deal," I said. "Go get that frozen yogurt with your kids and celebrate!"

"Will do," Liz said. "You should come! Please don't hide out in that empty hardware store all night!"

"Tell me when Callum leaves town, and I'll feel comfortable showing my face again."

When I hung up, my cheeks were sore from smiling so much with Liz. It was another moment when I thanked the universe for bringing such a great friend into my life.

"We'll find the right person," I told the store, feeling hope rise in my chest. "I know the right buyer is out there."

I stood from behind the desk and began walking down the closest aisle. I liked the ritual of walking from aisle to aisle before going home, imagining my dad doing this at the end of a long day. As a kid, I always wondered why he did it. Was he checking if anything was stolen or looking for broken shelves? But when I was older, I finally asked him.

"Why do you always walk all the aisles before you leave?"

I remembered the way my dad had shrugged beneath his baseball cap.

"Gives me time to think," he answered, as if trying to brush aside the question. But then he took a moment to think more deeply about it and looked thoughtfully at me before continuing. "A lot of people worked hard to make this place what it is. I like to spend a little time thinking about that."

And so, after my dad was gone, I reenacted the ritual. I walked aisle to aisle, guided by the bright fluorescent lights humming above me, and thought about my dad. I liked to run my hands along the shelves, checking that items were lined up properly even though no customers had entered the space for nearly a year.

I was in the last aisle, shifting my thoughts to dinner and what I had in my freezer to defrost, when I heard the ding of the front door. The sound surprised me. I hadn't heard the bell over the door for months, and my heart beat faster as I raced through all the possibilities of who might come through that door.

"Sorry, we're not open," I called out as I rounded the aisle to meet whoever it was at the front door.

Of all the possibilities I thought about and the people I pictured, I never imagined that Callum Jones would be standing at the front door of my dad's hardware store, smirking at me.

4

CALLUM

"What do you recommend for a leaky faucet?"

My attempt at a joke fell flat with Darcy, who stood at the end of an aisle, blinking at me. She looked shocked and possibly angry that I had burst into the store.

"What are you doing here?" Darcy asked. In truth, I was wondering that myself. While I knew this place belonged to Darcy's family, I hadn't expected her to be here. My own surprise and excitement over seeing her left me scrambling for what to say.

"I saw the 'For Sale' sign in the window," I explained, pointing back toward it.

"And so ... you came inside?" she asked, clearly questioning my level of common sense. I felt my cheeks flush in embarrassment. This was a new feeling for me. It was rare I couldn't charm my way out of a situation like this, but something about Darcy kept me tongue-tied and confused, like a teenager all over again.

"No, I know that's not an invitation to come in," I explained. "But my grandfather used to take me here all the time as a kid. And I suddenly wanted to see it. And when the door was open, it seemed like a sign."

I watched Darcy's shoulders relax and something soften in her eyes. God, she was beautiful. Those large green eyes were taking me in carefully, as if finally looking at me for the first time. I had an impulse to brush the hair back from my forehead, but I kept my hands firmly at my sides.

"I didn't know your grandfather lived in town," Darcy said. She tucked her long blonde hair behind her ear, and I smirked as I remembered the gesture. At the open house she had looked so professional in her blazer, so different from the girl I remembered. But she had taken off her blazer and rolled up her sleeves, so she looked much more casual and comfortable here in the hardware store. It made me breathe a little easier, feeling more comfortable too.

"Not anymore," I said, sliding my hands into the front pockets of my jeans. "He died when I was eleven. Liz would have been nine, so it was probably before you knew each other."

"How do you know when Liz and I met?" she asked, and I felt warmth flush through me as she smiled at me.

"I pay attention!" I said, laughing with her. "Fourth grade, right? Was it a softball team?"

"Soccer," Darcy said, her eyebrows lifting. "But I'm impressed."

There was a moment of quiet between us where I simply took Darcy in, waiting to see if she would say anything else. I knew I should probably leave. I had barged into the hardware store and found her alone. Clearly, she wasn't looking for company if she was inside a closed store with the shades covering the front windows. But she was staring at me, and I couldn't help wondering what she was thinking.

"Well, go ahead and look around," Darcy said, gesturing down the closest aisle. "If you want to."

She turned away and headed toward the front desk. I watched as she walked back to her seat and sorted through a stack of mail. The task in front of her seemed to take her full attention, and once again I wondered if I should leave. But something about Darcy's expression as she invited me to look around the store, a slight glint in her eye, kept me there. I made my way down the aisle closest to the checkout, where I could still talk to Darcy and hope to catch her looking over at me.

"I'm sorry about the open house," I said as I gently touched the paint rollers and brushes that decorated the aisle. I had a flash of Darcy at the open house, hands on her hips when she came through the doorway to check out the commotion my presence had caused. I remembered her shocked expression and how silly I felt with all the fans clamoring for my attention. That public persona, the celebrity musician, wasn't the image I wanted to show her.

"I thought I'd have some relief from being recognized here. But I guess it was too much to hope I could just be a normal guy."

She was still staring at the papers on the desk, and I wondered if she was even listening. But then she glanced over, looking at me sideways.

"When your band plays on *Saturday Night Live* I think it's kind of hard to go back to being 'normal'."

"You saw that?" I hated the eagerness and desperation in my voice. Why did I care if she saw my band on some late-night TV show?

Because it was a big deal, I said to myself. I was proud our music could speak to so many people. Maybe, if Darcy had taken the time to watch the show, she was someone our music resonated with. This was the whole reason I loved music: it could speak to people and, I hoped, make them feel less alone.

"I saw a clip-on Instagram," Darcy said, but she was looking away again and her voice sounded bored. My hope that Darcy liked our music quickly evaporated.

"Anyway, I didn't mean to derail the open house. I hope it didn't hurt business or anything like that."

"Don't worry, Liz got three offers on the place—one of them way over asking."

"Congratulations!" I said, smiling at her. "She's always been a persuasive saleswoman."

"Remember when she sold those school candy bars for two dollars instead of one and pocketed the profit?"

"I had forgotten that!" I laughed as I remembered the crumpled-up one-dollar bills Liz would pull from her backpack during the school fundraiser.

"She tried to sell them to my friends for *three* dollars. And some of them actually did it!"

This was one thing we could comfortably talk about: Liz. My sister had always been a social butterfly, pulling people together wherever she went. It was no surprise she was doing it now, even when she wasn't in the room.

As Darcy laughed, I felt the tension between us melt away. I felt comfortable enough to abandon my walk down the aisle and cross over to the desk where Darcy was sitting.

"Seems like the real estate business is going well. You've done a lot since the last time I saw you."

"Well, not as much as you." The way she smiled at me, just one corner of her mouth turned up, made my stomach flip. "You, the international sensation, and all that."

"*Accidental* sensation," I corrected. "Sometimes I wish I could give it all back."

"You don't want to pursue music anymore?" She looked interested, as if she truly wanted to know the answer. So often people seemed frustrated with me for questioning the rock-star life. Inevitably, they would point out the perks of traveling the world and having money. They didn't want to hear someone complain about it. But something in me wondered if Darcy might actually understand.

"I love music. It's all the other stuff I'm not thrilled about. The talk shows and the meet and greets. And all the pressure to keep going, to make more music, to book more shows. Sometimes it feels like the success of the band is all on *my* shoulders."

Wondering if Darcy would think this all a bit self-centered, I feared coming off as conceited or selfish. Pointing out that I wrote all the band's music on top of being the lead singer sometimes made people think I was simply trying to show off. But there was a softness in Darcy's eyes that told me she was trying to understand. I saw compassion there, and an understanding that felt different from the way other people regarded me.

Standing there, connecting like that, something in the air seemed to change between us. My eyes locked with hers, and I couldn't mistake the pull I felt between us. Desperate to get closer, I took a step forward. A moment of surprise passed across her face, but then desire appeared, a longing and excitement reflected in my own body. My eyes dropped to her lips, showing her that I wanted to kiss her.

Suddenly, the overhead fluorescent lights clicked off, plunging the store into darkness. Darcy's gaze shot up to the ceiling, and I stepped back. Though it was still daytime outside, the shades along the large storefront windows were closed, allowing very little sunlight to filter into the room.

"Must be a fuse," Darcy said. "The lights have been tripping lately."

She seemed almost relieved by the distraction, and she set off toward the back of the store, pushing her way through a door that said, "Staff Only". On a whim, I followed her. I was pretty sure she didn't need my help, but the promise of that kiss was still in my mind, and I wasn't ready to abandon it so quickly.

The hallway was dark, and I watched Darcy feel her way along the wall. I pulled out my cell phone and flipped on the flashlight feature, holding it up to illuminate her path.

"Thanks," she said over her shoulder. We passed a doorway on the left that looked like an office and continued to the end of the hallway where Darcy opened a small door. It was a utility closet from the look of things, filled with mops and brooms, with the fuse box on the wall.

Darcy stepped inside and opened the fuse box, but it was too dark to clearly see the different switches.

"Can you bring the flashlight over here?" she asked. I stepped inside the closet with her and stood directly behind her. The space was so small we were nearly touching, but I aimed the flashlight over Darcy's shoulder so she could see what she was doing.

Standing here, inches away from her, I felt my whole body tense. I couldn't help imagining what it would feel like to step forward, to let Darcy lean back into my chest and feel my whole body pressed against hers. In the comfort of the dark, I had an impulse to brush her hair aside so I could kiss the back of her neck.

Stop that, I told myself, shaking the thoughts aside.

Despite the look in Darcy's eyes at the counter, I didn't know what she was feeling about me. I needed to calm myself down before I made a fool of myself.

With the flashlight showing the way, Darcy quickly found the tripped fuse and flipped it back. We saw the lights in the hallway click on and heard the hum of electricity overhead. Darcy turned around with a smile, proud of herself, but all at once she seemed to realize how close we were to one another. The smile slowly faded from her face and I thought I could read a question, and maybe an invitation, in her eyes.

When Darcy bit her bottom lip ever so slightly, I couldn't help myself. I bent down to put my lips against hers and brought a hand up to squeeze the top of Darcy's arm. She responded immediately, pressing back and bringing her hand to my waist. My heart beat faster as we stepped closer together and then I deepened the kiss, opening my mouth slightly, inviting her in.

She had seemed timid, but now she embraced the kiss. I felt her relax, and a small sigh escaped from her as the kiss deepened. I brought my hand up to Darcy's neck, the very place I had imagined kissing moments earlier. As I cupped her head in my hand, my fingers moved up into her hair. I relished the intimacy of the moment and the way Darcy seemed to press back into my hand even as she opened her mouth further to me.

I was shocked when she moved forward and closed the gap between us, pressing her full body against me.

"Darcy," I whispered, wanting nothing more than to get closer. I needed more of her. I pressed back against her eager body and walked her to the wall, putting my hand behind her back to protect her from the hard metal of the fuse box. There was fire in her eyes, and I met her lips again, matching the passion Darcy was showing me.

But just as I started kissing her again, Darcy pushed me aside, both hands pushing hard against my chest.

"I have to go," she said as I stepped back. Darcy slipped out of the closet, leaving me blinking as the light from the hallway filtered into the small space.

5

DARCY

I stood at the counter, my heart pounding as I sorted through mail for maybe the tenth time that day. Callum was going to think I couldn't read or something. But it was the only thing I could find to look occupied with when Callum walked out from the back hallway.

For the second time that day I had run away from him. I felt my cheeks flush with embarrassment as the door behind me swung open. I kept my eyes down, unable to look at him.

"Darcy," he said. Without warning a wave of desire flushed through me as I remembered the way he had whispered my name in the back closet. He crossed in front of the counter, and I was glad to have the large desk between us.

"Is everything okay?"

"Sorry," I said, though I kicked myself for apologizing. It felt like I had spent all day trying to make amends for my actions.

"Did I ...? I'm sorry if I misread something back there."

"Don't worry about it," I said. My eyes were still on the mail. It felt too strange to meet his gaze. The truth was, I didn't even know why I had run. Kissing Callum had felt good. Maybe *too* good. When I felt his body press up against me, all thoughts seemed to fly out of my head. I only felt desire and longing, stronger than I had in a long time. It left me feeling confused and overwhelmed. And I had to get out of there. I had spent nearly ten years hating Callum Jones. I couldn't let one afternoon with him erase all our history together.

"I really am sorry," Callum said. There was confusion in his voice, and I glanced up to see him run his hand over his face, as if washing away our encounter. Was he upset? I wanted to explain all the things I was feeling, but I couldn't figure out how to form words.

"I just got out of a relationship," I blurted out. When I was cornered in a bar, some guy begging to buy me a drink, this had become my go-to response. If some client asked me to dinner, I always had it in my back pocket to let them down easy. I wasn't sure why I was pulling this excuse out for Callum when, in reality, all I wanted was to reach across the counter and pull him back in for another kiss. But it felt like something that might excuse my strange behavior back there.

"Right," Callum said, and it sounded like he might know the story. I made a mental note to yell at Liz for telling her brother about my failed engagement.

"I'm not in a place to jump into something else right now."

"Of course. I get it."

"Plus, my dad passed away."

Oh my god, why are you telling him all of this? It was like I had no control over what was coming out of my mouth. All I wanted was to sink into the floor behind the counter and disappear.

"Liz told me about that. I'm so sorry." For a moment I thought he might come around the counter to put a hand on my back or try to hug me. But before he could, I walked away, intent on keeping as much space between us as possible.

"It's alright," I said, as I rearranged empty flowerpots that were perfectly fine where they were. I just needed something to keep me busy until Callum took the hint and left me alone.

"Look, I'm playing a show tonight at the Music Hall. I'd love it if you came."

The gentleness in his voice made me look up at him despite my determination to do anything but. I was touched he wanted me to come to his concert.

"I set it up so my manager would let me come home. He's *always* looking for opportunities to get my name out there and play more shows. But it's just me—no band. So, I'm trying out some of my acoustic stuff."

As he spoke, I recognized a tentative excitement in his voice, as if the idea of performing on his own was something he was looking forward to. Did I also sense some nerves? I had to admit I was interested to see what the show would look like. I was familiar with the loud and energetic shows he usually played with his band. Seeing Callum alone onstage with his guitar would be a much more intimate experience.

"Sounds like you're excited about it," I guessed, and I saw a genuine smile spread across his face.

"Excited but scared," he said, and I was pleased with myself for picking up on those emotions so clearly.

"You've performed in like a hundred countries," I laughed. "How are you scared?"

"It's different when I'm on my own. I don't have the band

and all the loud music to hide behind. Anyway, it would be great if you came."

I looked at him, trying not to let my eyes drop to those full lips that had been kissing me only moments ago. Every time I tried to remember why I didn't like Callum Jones, I found myself being drawn to him again. He was being so kind to me and seemed genuinely interested ...

That's exactly what you thought last time, I told myself. As a teenager, I had thought he cared about me. But he had proved otherwise. Plus, there were all those girls I saw him photographed with on the covers of magazines. Callum Jones had his pick of women. There was no way he was seriously interested in *me*.

"Maybe," I said. I wasn't ready to commit, but I was also trying to get him out of the store.

"Liz will be there." It was clear from his eager expression that he wanted me to say yes. If that was what it took to get him out of the store, I would do it.

"Alright, fine," I said. "I'll be there."

"Great." His smile seemed genuine. I watched him push the hair out of his eyes and wondered if he was going to say something else. But then he nodded and cocked his head toward the door.

"I'll get out of here. See you tonight."

"Yeah. See you tonight."

I followed him to the front door so I could lock it behind him. The last thing I needed was any more unexpected guests wandering into the store. On the sidewalk, Callum smiled at me before turning right and heading back into town. I breathed a sigh of relief as I watched him walk away.

With an irrational fear that Callum might change his mind and come back, I rushed back to the counter to grab my purse and my blazer before returning to the front door. I closed it and locked it, turning both the lock and the dead bolt just to be sure. I checked down the street and saw the figure of Callum getting smaller and smaller in the distance. And then, making a break for it, I rushed across the street to our real estate office.

I pushed my way through the door with the colorful 'Dream Home Realty' logo we had recently revamped. I felt a strange sense of panic as I closed it as quickly as I could and turned the dead bolt behind me.

"What'd you do, rob a bank?"

I spun around, shocked to hear someone behind me. Liz sat at her desk, papers set up all around her and an iced coffee in her hand.

"My god, I thought you left," I said.

"I wanted to get this paperwork finished up. Eric's picking up the kids. Why do you look so spooked?"

"Nothing," I said, crossing to my own desk. But I knew Liz wouldn't let me off the hook that easily. As I slumped down into my chair, the whole story came tumbling out.

"Callum came into the store. I don't even know how he found it or how he knew I was in there, but things got … interesting."

"What does *that* mean?" Liz rolled her office chair over to my desk as I dropped my head into my hands.

"We kissed," I groaned through my fingers. I heard Liz squeal in excitement next to me.

"That was fast! How did that happen?"

"I don't even know! We were talking and suddenly, he was right there in front of me, looking adorable. And then the lights went out in the place, and we had to find the fuse box. And he was just *there*, right behind me. It just happened."

"This is amazing!"

"No, it's not. I ran away from him *again*. I literally pushed him away from me and *ran away*."

"Oh, Darcy ..."

"I know. He must think I'm a total freak."

"What did he say?"

"Nothing! Of course, he was the one apologizing. I couldn't even look at him."

"I'm sure it wasn't that bad."

"I don't know what I'm doing, Liz." I said, turning to her. I felt like I might explode if I didn't figure out all the feeling swirling inside of me. "The man's a celebrity. It's not like he's looking for something long-term. He has his pick of whatever woman he wants."

"Callum's not like that," Liz said, but I brushed this aside. Of course, Liz would say that.

"I don't know ..."

"It sounds like something else is bothering you."

I sighed. Liz was always so perceptive. Sometimes she seemed to know my thoughts before I knew them myself.

"I know it's stupid, but I can't stop thinking about high school. He was a total *jerk*. I know it was ages ago, but am I just supposed to forget all about it?"

"You could talk to him about it," Liz suggested, but the idea of bringing up some incident from so many years ago made me feel sick. Liz could read it on my face, and she quickly tried to change the subject.

"You need to get out and have some fun. You've been wrapped up in work and all the stuff with John and your dad for *months*. Callum has a concert tonight—why don't you come along? We can have a girl's night!"

"He already invited me." I couldn't believe I had agreed to go. After kissing the man only to push him away, I didn't know how I would face him tonight without dying from embarrassment. I wondered if I could sneak out before the concert was over. I began running through excuses in my mind, working out what might be a reasonable excuse for going home early.

"You have to come!" Liz said, but I was distracted, too busy imagining what the night might be like. I felt Liz's hand on my shoulder as she gave me a good-natured shove. "Don't think about things so much."

"Easy for you to say," I laughed. "I don't know if I should go."

"Just relax, Dar. Callum's staying for the summer and, since he's my brother and you're my best friend, chances are you'll have to interact a bit. Maybe you can just have some fun?"

I had to admit that *fun* was one of the last adjectives I would use to describe the past year of my life. Maybe Liz was right. He was only here for a few months. Would it be so bad to let myself relax a little bit?

"Alright," I said, letting myself feel a bit of excitement about the night ahead. "I'll go."

Liz squealed again, and I felt my spirits rise as I thought about a fun night out with Liz. It had been ages since we'd been out for more than a quick dinner or drink after work. With Liz's kids and my attention on the business, we hadn't had a real night out together in a long time.

"Let's go," Liz said, gathering her things from her desk.

"Where are we going?"

"Shopping!"

6

CALLUM

"Thank you, Maplewood!" I said, smiling across the theater. "I can't tell you how good it feels to be back home."

I took a deep breath as I looked out to the crowd. So far, I had played some of the Horizon's most successful singles. Members of the audience sang along, excited to know every word. But I was at the point in the concert where I planned to debut some of my new music. I felt overwhelmed with nerves as I began, momentarily wondering if I should abandon the idea entirely. But I made myself push forward.

"I'm going to do something a bit different if you'll allow me," I said. I swallowed hard and tried to ignore my heart beating out of my chest. "I've been working on some new music. And I thought I would share some of it with you all tonight."

Grateful that the stage lights blocked most of their faces, I could only see people in the first few rows of the theater. A tense moment of silence hung in the air as I looked out, listening to see how they would react to this news. And then, thankfully, the crowd cheered from their seats in the old theater. Thank God they were still with me. I just hoped they would still be cheering when the new songs were finished.

I had a simple setup onstage: just a microphone, my guitar, and a stool. I sat down now and brought the microphone closer to my mouth. And then, I started to play.

This is crazy, I told myself as the first line of the lyrics flowed out of me. *You haven't let a soul hear this song. And now you're debuting it in front of a crowd of 500 people.*

But as I sang, the song overtook me. I lost all sense of self-consciousness or fear. There was something about singing a song you had created. Something about performing something that had come from inside of you. It was a feeling I would never get over. I could only hope the crowd would feel the same love and embrace the songs I was sharing with them.

Is she out there?

Even with all the nerves coursing through me and the adrenaline of performing a new song, my mind drifted to Darcy. The question of whether she would come had been running through my head all evening. Was Darcy Stevens in the crowd? Performing in my hometown meant I had tons of friends and family here, but there was only one person I cared about right now.

Earlier, when I arrived at the theater, I was so distracted I barely made it through sound check. The audio engineer kept asking if I could hear myself in the monitors and if I needed the levels adjusted. But it wasn't any technical challenges that had my thoughts floating out into space. It was Darcy.

I couldn't stop thinking about that kiss in the supply closet and the way her warm lips pressed against mine, eager for more. If I closed my eyes, I could still feel the desperate way she held my shirt in her fist and pulled me closer. I could still feel her whole body pressed against mine as I struggled to be closer to her. And yet, she had pushed me away.

What made her stop? I asked myself.

Despite these distractions, I made it through my set. I felt a flush of pride as the crowd gave a standing ovation and even asked for an encore. Maybe this new music had been alright. After the show, I stood in the lobby to thank the audience. I hadn't done that since some of the earliest concerts the Horizon gave. But I wanted to thank the people of my hometown for coming to see me, and I knew there would be plenty of friends who wanted to say hello.

"Oh my God, Callum, it was amazing!" Liz cried out, wrapping her arms around me. I had been talking to a fan, someone who insisted we knew each other in high school, though I had no memory of the guy. So I was grateful when Liz launched herself at me to hang her arms around my neck. It was just the hint the talkative fan needed to excuse himself.

"That new music!" Liz cried. "I think it's your best yet!" She released her arms from my neck and nearly stumbled as she stepped away from me. I had to laugh at her.

"Someone's having fun," I said. I didn't miss the strong smell of alcohol on my sister's breath.

"Oh, hush," Liz said, swatting my shoulder. "It's been a long time since I've been out without the kids. I'm allowed to relax a bit."

"I'm glad you enjoyed yourself," I smiled. I felt a sudden burst of warmth toward Liz. We had been distant for several years while I pursued music and toured the world. But after only a few days with Liz, I realized just how much I had missed her.

Another person came up to shake my hand, and I spent a moment with her. As I posed for a selfie with the girl, I couldn't help scanning the room, searching for someone.

"She's here," Liz said, giving a smirk that told me she knew exactly who I was looking for. "She got trapped by this client we have who has *insane* requirements for her house. I swear she has no intention of actually buying a home. She just likes talking to us."

"Who do you mean?" I asked, playing dumb, but Liz wouldn't even entertain my question.

"I can't believe you kissed her!" Liz whispered. But in her slightly intoxicated state, this whisper was closer to a full-blown conversation.

"*Liz!*" I scolded. Luckily the people around us seemed occupied with their own conversations. But there were too many people milling about the lobby for Liz to be spreading something like that around. I knew firsthand how rumors could explode into problems very quickly.

"It's nothing to be embarrassed about!" Liz said.

"*I'm* not embarrassed," I said. "But I'm not sure Darcy wants it talked about all over town."

"That's just Darcy," Liz laughed. "Always second-guessing her decisions. I love her, but the girl doesn't know what's good for her!"

Just then, I caught sight of Darcy pressing her way through the crowd. I felt a jolt in my stomach at the sight of her. She wore tight black jeans and a sequined tank top that gave her a rock-concert edge I wasn't expecting. With her dark eyeliner and heeled boots, she would have fit in at any Horizon concert. My eyes dropped to those soft lips, and I was once again in the supply closet, hearing Darcy sigh as I kissed her.

"Doesn't she look *amazing?*" Liz squealed as Darcy joined us. "We went shopping!"

"It's a good look," I agreed, enjoying the invitation to stare. I caught Darcy's eyes and smiled at her, but she looked away and focused on Liz.

"She was so excited about putting together 'a look'," Darcy said.

"You have to have *the look*!" Liz protested. "Ask any of those groupies who follow him across the world. You have to dress right for a Callum Jones concert."

"I don't have groupies," I said, shaking my head. The last thing I wanted was Darcy to think I went around sleeping with women and taking advantage of my fame.

"Oh! Who wants drinks?" Liz asked. She had caught sight of the bar in the lobby and clearly wasn't ready for the evening to end.

"Liz, they're trying to clean up," I said, taking hold of my sister's arm before she could float away. "Come back to my dressing room and we'll have a drink."

This solution seemed acceptable for Liz because she took off back into the theater, expecting us to follow her.

"I think your sister needs to get out more," Darcy laughed, raising her eyebrows as Liz practically skipped down the aisle.

"I think you're right," I agreed. I was glad to share a smile with Darcy and glad to walk so close to her. Our shoulders nearly touched as we walked down the aisle and ducked into an alcove at the side of the stage.

"This way." I held a curtain aside for Darcy and let her cross in front of me. I called Liz over from where she was dancing on the stage and nodded toward the staircase. Soon, we were all heading down the steps toward the dressing rooms.

"Watch your head," I warned as we descended the old theater staircase. The architecture of this place meant that I had to duck to avoid a pipe that cut across the ceiling.

The theater was a historic space, built sometime in the 1800s and, despite numerous renovations, it didn't have many of the amenities I had become accustomed to on tour. Not that I minded. I didn't need much. They had given me the largest dressing room available, but the place was tiny compared to the large and sometimes multi-room spaces I was often given. But this place had charm, and I found it more comfortable than some of the famous arenas I had performed in.

"Go ahead," I said, letting Darcy into the space. It had a counter along one wall with mirrors running across it. The other side had a couch that someone had decorated with colorful throw pillows to brighten the room. The only other thing in the room was a small sink tucked into a corner and a doorless closet space for costumes and clothing.

"Sorry for the tight fit," I said as the three of us squeezed into the space. The venue had left me a bottle of scotch (likely something Brady had written into my contract), and I unstacked three plastic cups onto the counter so I could pour.

"The songs were wonderful, Cal," Liz declared again as I handed out the shots.

"They really were," agreed Darcy. My head whipped around at Darcy's compliment, and our eyes met as I smiled at her.

"I'm glad you liked it," I said. I was surprised to realize how true those words were. Hearing Darcy approve of the new music felt more important than any future record executive's opinion.

"To a good summer," I said, lifting my plastic cup in the air.

"To a good summer," Liz and Darcy repeated. We knocked our cups together and drank. I felt the scotch warm and harsh as it burned its way down my throat. Next time, I would ask Brady to specify something a bit closer to the top shelf.

"It's past my bedtime," Liz announced, slamming her cup onto the counter.

"I thought you wanted to drink!" I laughed. Liz's whims often amused me as she floated from one thought to the next.

"We drank!" she exclaimed, gesturing to the scotch. For the second time that night, Liz wrapped her arms around my neck. "Congratulations," she said. Her hug was warm and genuine, and I hugged her back firmly. I was trying to thank her for all the support she had given me since coming home.

"I'll drive you home," Darcy said, gathering her purse, but Liz shook her head.

"Eric's outside for me." I didn't know Liz's husband well, but from everything I knew, Eric was a devoted husband who cared about Liz. That made him good in my book.

Liz gave Darcy a hug before putting a hand on her cheek in an affectionate gesture.

"Stay and have another drink," Liz insisted. Something seemed to pass between the two of them, but I couldn't work out what it might mean. All at once, Liz was bouncing out of the dressing room, leaving Darcy and me alone in the small space.

"Well," I said, shaking my head. I felt like we had just survived a Liz-shaped tornado, quickly touching down before evaporating just as quickly. "Another drink?"

"Why not?" Darcy replied, and her laugh was relaxed and friendly. I had expected her to excuse herself politely and slip out of the room. Instead, she had opted to stay, even taking a seat on the couch. I wasn't about to question it. I poured a new round of drinks and walked them over to her.

"Thanks." Darcy's hand reached up to take the cup. She looked at me carefully as our hands touched in the handoff. What was she thinking? I sat down on the couch beside her and sipped the cheap alcohol, waiting.

"How do you feel?" Darcy asked. She pulled a leg up onto the couch so she could turn to face me.

"About the show?" I turned to her as well, settling into a more comfortable position. The couch was so small our knees almost touched. What would happen if I shifted forward a bit? If I allowed my knee to touch hers?

"Yeah. After a show ... do you feel excited? Or more of a letdown?"

The cheap alcohol was already going to my head. I felt warm and relaxed as I rested my arm along the back of the couch. I always felt both satisfied and eager after a show, filled with a buzz unlike any other.

"Depends," I shrugged. I took in the slight smile on her face and the pink flush on her cheeks.

"On what?"

I swallowed, downing my cup. Was there an invitation in her eyes? I took a breath and considered her carefully before answering.

"It depends on how the show went. And, once the show's over, if I have someone special to celebrate with."

7

DARCY

I felt my stomach flip at Callum's words.

"Someone to celebrate with?" I asked, teasing him. "Is that what we're doing?"

There was a flash in Callum's eyes, though whether it was shock or desire I couldn't tell. He nodded as his eyes slightly narrowed in my direction.

"Yes," he said. "I would say we're celebrating."

The logical part of my brain told me I should get out of there. It was too warm and comfortable in this small room, and the man across from me was far too handsome. If I stayed we would probably pick up right where we left off in that storage room. But I was finding it all too easy to ignore that logical side of my brain.

Maybe you can just have some fun.

Liz's words ran over and over in my head. Is that what I was doing? Having fun with Callum Jones? I looked across the couch to see Callum staring at me. What was he thinking? I felt pulled toward him, and all I could imagine was leaning forward to press my lips into his own.

Stop that, I told myself. But the image wouldn't leave my mind.

A slight lean would press my knee into his ... another few inches to close the gap ...

No, I needed to break this spell. Forcing my eyes down to the plastic cup in my hand, I gulped my drink and tried to ignore the man across from me. But this move was disastrous. The alcohol burned my throat and caused a coughing fit that brought tears to my eyes.

"Are you alright?" Callum asked. He was up on his feet, filling a cup with water to bring over to me.

"My God, this stuff is bad," I laughed through my coughing. I took the water from him and set the scotch on the ground.

"Sorry," Callum said. "Usually, it's a bit more ... expensive."

"I guess you can't expect much in Maplewood," I laughed. With the mood in the room lighter, Callum resumed his seat on the couch. I didn't miss the fact he sat closer to me to let his knee touch mine. I also didn't make any effort to move.

"I like this look," Callum said, and I saw his eyes on my hair, my earrings, the makeup around my eyes. I tried not to squirm under his gaze.

"It was Liz," I said. "She wanted us to look like part of your entourage."

"My entourage?" he asked.

"Fans. Groupies. From all the pictures, you don't seem to lack for admirers."

"You've seen pictures?" Callum asked. I felt a flush of embarrassment as I chewed my bottom lip, embarrassed to have been found out.

"It's not like I'm stalking you or anything."

"I'm not with those girls, you know." Callum said, and I saw him lean in slightly, shifting his arm closer to mine on the couch.

"What?"

"Any girls you see in those pictures. I'm not sleeping with them."

"Oh," I said. Once again, my body flushed as I heard Callum talk about sleeping with someone. He smirked at me, as if he could tell he was making me squirm. But I didn't mind. In fact, I felt an overwhelming desire to hear more about this. What sort of relationships did Callum Jones have?

"I don't believe you," I said, and it was my turn to smile as Callum's eyebrows flew up at my accusation. "It's hard to believe you spend too many nights on your own."

I put my arm on the back of the couch, and I was pleased when Callum understood the gesture. His hand was suddenly touching mine, making small circles on the back of my hand.

"You think I'm lying?" he asked. I could feel my heart-beat in the depths of my stomach, creeping lower to bring heat between my legs. God, I was playing with fire. But Liz's reminder to have some fun kept running through my head.

"I'm not sure," I said, answering truthfully. "But I can imagine there are times after a show, when the right person is around …"

I could hardly recognize myself. Who was this girl challenging and enticing the man sitting in front of her? It was thrilling to speak so boldly to him, to play the part of someone much more outspoken and confident. This was a woman who wanted something, and she was figuring out how to ask for it.

"The right person …" Callum repeated.

I watched desire flood into his eyes as Callum closed the gap between us. He dropped his mouth to mine, and I felt his hand grip hard on my forearm still on the back of the couch. His other hand found my knee, and he squeezed it as he pressed his mouth hard against mine. I opened my mouth to him, feeling the comfortable buzz of alcohol coursing through my veins, which made me more attuned to the pleasure running through me.

I moaned as I felt Callum's tongue flick across my own.

"God, Darcy," he gasped. He pulled away to look me in the eye, and I saw my own hunger reflected there. I needed to be closer to him, to feel more of him. I sat up on my knees and Callum moved both feet to the floor so I could straddle him. A shiver ran through me as his hands slid to my thighs.

"God, yes," he whispered. Callum pressed his hips up to me, and I could feel his growing hardness between my legs. It made me press against him with need, pleased to feel what I was doing to him. I kissed him as Callum's firm hands on my thighs rocked me back and forth across his lap. Soon I had the rhythm all on my own, and Callum brought one hand to my ass while the other moved to my chest.

He felt me up through my shirt, first one breast and then the other, but it wasn't enough. If I was going to be bold tonight, I would show this man exactly what I wanted. I took his hand and guided it to the hem of my shirt, wanting to feel Callum's hand on me without the boundary of fabric. He obliged, running his hand up my stomach and then up to my bra. I gasped as his finger dipped down to circle my nipple, giving me exactly what I wanted.

I could feel warmth pooling between my legs as I pressed myself against him. His fingers on my nipples made me lightheaded, almost unable to keep up my passionate kissing. Shocks of pleasure were like lightning bolts all the way down to my toes. With a quick move, Callum slid an arm around my back and lifted me to lay me flat on my back on the couch.

"I *really* like this look," Callum said again as he stared down at me, his voice breathless and deep. With conviction, he dropped to take my mouth in his own. He had one knee between my legs, and I couldn't help squeezing against him as he kissed me.

His hand was once more at the hem of my shirt, but this time I sat up and flipped it over my head. Then I slid my hands beneath Callum's tight T-shirt, and in one swift move, it was off and cast to the floor. God, it felt good to put my hands on his smooth, broad chest. I pulled him down to me, wanting to feel his skin against my own.

I could feel Callum's length straining beneath his jeans as I pressed my thigh into him. I was desperate to feel more. His mouth dipped down to my breast as his hand pulled aside my bra, and I felt his tongue press warm and hard against my nipple. I cried out at this contact, a spark of heat running straight from my breast to the place between my legs. I saw his eyes flick up to mine, a devilish grin on his face as he saw how much pleasure he was bringing me. In response, I reached up to release my bra to the floor, inviting Callum to have access.

As he played, I kissed his neck and even let my teeth nip at his jawline and his ear. From the gentle growls I heard, I could only imagine he was enjoying it. His hand snaked down my stomach, and I heard a soft pop as he expertly undid the button of my jeans. Callum lowered the zipper and then played his fingers around the top of my underwear.

"Callum," I gasped, desperate for his touch. I knew how eager I was for him.

"Tell me what you need," he growled into my ear.

"Please ..." Darcy asked. "Please touch me."

He slid his fingers down and quickly dipped into my wetness, surprising me with the speed of it. I was soaked for him, and Callum drew his finger up and down as I gasped. He tucked his head into my neck and focused on pleasuring me. He increased his speed and brought his mouth back to my breasts, licking and sucking as his fingers began a rhythm that threatened to undo me.

"Keep going," I cried, feeling tension build between my legs. I held onto Callum's back as his fingers circled that most sensitive spot, driving me higher into pleasure. I closed my eyes and felt my body tense. His tongue circled my nipple as his fingers circled below, and I was soon crying out, exploding over the top of desire.

"Good girl," Callum growled, and I could feel his smile against my chest. I couldn't move. Pleasure was coursing through me, and I wanted to ride it. But there was more to explore, and after a moment I turned my eyes back to Callum, asking a silent question. He stood up from the couch, and I saw his dark eyes staring at me as he leaned back down and brought his hands to the waistband of my jeans. With a strong pull, he peeled the tight jeans off me, leaving me naked in front of him.

I delighted in the possessive look Callum gave as his eyes scanned my naked body. I allowed myself the same boldness as I watched Callum undo his belt and drop his jeans to the ground, sliding jeans and briefs in one go. My breath caught in my throat as I saw the hard length of him, eager and ready. He put a hand out to me and I eagerly took hold.

With decisive strength, he pulled me to standing, and then dragged my body to press against his own. I shivered as I felt every inch of him and felt his erection pressing between us. I expected him to be rough, but Callum kissed me sweetly, cupping my cheeks with both hands to draw my face closer to him.

"I want you," he whispered. Callum's kiss became more insistent, and he spun us so he could walk me backward to the other side of the room. I walked blindly, claiming his lips as we moved, until my ass bumped into the countertop. Callum's hands slid down to my waist, and I let him lift me a few inches until I was resting on top of it. I gasped as I saw Callum's hand between his legs. I couldn't look away as he guided himself toward me. He stared at me, eyes locked, as he found my opening and rested there.

"Tell me what you need," Callum said again. I was too desperate to have any sense of shame.

"Take me, please," I said, ready to beg if I had to. Luckily, Callum did not make me wait. He thrust forward and entered me, pushing my back into the cold mirror behind me. I cried out as I felt the full length of him stretching inside me. As he moved, Callum dipped his mouth down to kiss me. I brought my hands to his triceps, holding myself in place as Callum thrusts faster, sliding my body across the countertop.

"Oh, Callum," I cried out. I wrapped my legs around his upper thighs to hold tighter, giving him better purchase. I felt the strong muscles of his legs as he worked himself in and out of me.

"God, Darcy," he said. "You drive me crazy."

His rhythm increased, and I threw my head back against the mirror and simply tried to hold on, feeling pleasure course through my core as Callum took what he wanted.

"Darcy," Callum said again, and there was desperation in his voice as he let the primal part of him take control, losing himself in the sensations. With a groan I felt Callum pull out of me, and then another cry as he rested his forehead against my chest, gasping for breath. He stayed like this, recovering, and I brought my hands to his back. I caressed the back of his neck as we came down from our high together.

"You're wonderful," he said, turning his face up to me. He put a hand on my cheek and kissed me gently. The tenderness of it surprised me. And I was suddenly unsure about standing here, kissing Callum. Something about that affectionate gesture burst me out of the spell, and I felt a sudden unease in my stomach as I took in the reality of what had just happened.

With a shaky breath, I dropped my feet to the floor. As Callum stepped away, I stood up.

You're just like one of his groupies, I told myself. I wasn't sure I liked the title. I was suddenly aware of how much more experience Callum likely had with these sorts of casual flings than I did.

"I should go," I said, gathering my clothes from the ground to get dressed.

"Don't," he said, a lightness to his voice. "At least stay for another glass of horrible scotch."

"I have to be up early tomorrow," I said, glancing briefly at him. He seemed in no hurry to put his clothes on, and I felt my body flush all over again at the sight of him. I scrambled to gather my things and glanced at myself in the mirror. I was glad to see my eyeliner wasn't running and my hair wasn't too much of a mess.

"Will I see you tomorrow?"

I was kneeling to zip up my boot. I couldn't look at him. He was clearly saying what he thought I wanted to hear, a script he followed after all his casual flings. I wouldn't be part of the game or performance or whatever else he was playing.

"I know this was a onetime thing," I announced, standing and putting a hand on the door handle. I wouldn't let him think I was some naive girl expecting things from him. "You have a whole life on the road, and you're not about to settle down. So, it's alright. We don't have to pretend this was anything more than it was."

With that, I pushed my way out the door. I tried not to look, but I caught a flash of a shocked expression on Callum's face.

8

CALLUM

"Late night?"

I looked up from the breakfast table to see Liz entering. I was nursing a pounding headache as I cradled a coffee mug in my hands. I groaned at my sister, unable to form words. She smirked at me and went to pour a mug of her own.

I had barely slept. After Darcy walked out last night, I sat in my dressing room trying to figure out what had happened. The memory of our time together kept flashing through my brain, perfect and tantalizing. But then I saw Darcy standing at the door.

We don't have to pretend this was anything more than it was.

What had she meant? I couldn't figure out why things had changed so quickly. I thought there was a true connection between us. Something we were both recognizing. But after last night, I was pretty sure Darcy didn't feel the same way I did. And yet she had slept with me...

"What time did you get home?" Liz asked as she took a seat next to me.

"Maybe three?" I guessed.

After Darcy left, I got dressed and sat in front of the mirror. I stared at myself, trying to figure out what was going on. But every time I looked, my mind flashed to Darcy on the counter, her legs wrapped around me, her back pressed into the wall.

"And Darcy?" Liz asked. I wasn't in the mood for Liz's intrigue. And I definitely wasn't ready to tell my sister all the details of last night. If Darcy wanted Liz to know, she could tell her.

"Earlier," I grumbled. I left it at that. Let Liz think what she wanted.

Eventually, some custodian of the theater had come down to knock on the door and ask me to leave. I had snapped at the man, but I knew the cleaner wasn't the source of my frustration. How had I let things go so badly with Darcy?

"Where are the kids?" I asked, needing something else to talk about. I was used to energetic breakfasts with my niece and nephew fighting over the cereal box. This morning the house was quiet.

"We dropped them with the grandparents last night," Liz explained. "They love it, and it gives me and Eric a break."

I sipped my coffee black, glad for the hot liquid that burned its way down my throat.

"Hey, don't worry about Darcy." I kept my eyes on my mug as Liz spoke. The last thing I wanted was to talk to my sister about my sex life. My shoulders stiffened, and I had to force myself not to snap at Liz.

"She'll come around," Liz continued. "You know she was engaged, right?"

I remembered hearing this. Mostly because I remembered the strange sadness I had felt when I saw the engagement photos on Instagram. It had felt like the closing of a

58   EMMA REESE

door. So I was flooded with relief when one day on the phone Liz said she no longer had to help Darcy plan a wedding.

"And her father passed away. It's a lot for one person to deal with. All in the course of maybe eight months. So, I'm not surprised she isn't ready to jump into something new."

Darcy had told me both these things in the hardware store, but I didn't have many of the details.

"What happened with her fiancé?" I grumbled, letting my curiosity get the better of me. Liz's eyes grew wide as she slid closer to me.

"Don't tell her I said this, but I never liked the guy. He was the sort of dude who insisted on splitting checks at dinner and keeping tabs on who paid for the last tank of gas. Very...transactional."

I felt an instant dislike bubbling in my chest.

"No joke—he kept lists on who chose the TV show they would watch each night. And his workout schedule *always* trumped any plans they might have. Eric and I invited them to join us for a weekend vacation, and they couldn't come until Saturday morning because he had to go to the gym Friday night."

"Sounds like a selfish ass." If Liz's stories were true, it was a good thing Darcy had gotten away from this guy. She deserved better than a husband who wrapped himself up in his own interests. A question started banging in my head, joining the headache pressing against my eyes.

"Do you think ..." I stopped myself.

"What?" Liz asked. I debated whether I should talk to her about this. I remembered the way she would tease me about girlfriends when we were teenagers. But Liz and I were finding a nice adult relationship. Maybe she could bring some insight to the situation. After all, she was Darcy's best friend.

"Do you think Darcy sees me that way? Wrapped up only in myself?"

To her credit, Liz didn't laugh at me. But she also didn't deny it. I felt something hard and painful in my chest, growing worse the longer Liz let the silence hang between us.

"She *might* think that," Liz said carefully. "I think a lot of people might. All the news stories and the magazine articles ... those people like to show a certain image, you know?"

"I can't help what they write about me!" It was a constant frustration for me. When I wanted to focus on music, the world seemed more interested in my latest hairstyle and which girl was walking me into the concert venue.

"I know. But it's out there. Anyone reading about you is bound to assume you're some rock star looking for fame and women and money."

"But that's not me," I mumbled.

"*I* know that," Liz assured me. "Of course I do. But Darcy hasn't seen you since high school. You've barely talked to each other. All she's had are the news articles and the talk-show interviews."

"But don't you tell her? When you talk about me, don't you explain it's all an act?"

Now was the time for Liz to laugh. She snorted, rolling her eyes at me.

"Despite what you might think, we don't spend much time chatting about my older brother. God, maybe this rock-star role *has* gone to your head."

"That's not what I meant," I said. But I had to admit it was a bit crazy to think Liz and Darcy sat around talking about me.

"It's alright," Liz said. "I know you're not like that."

We sipped coffee together, enjoying each other's company.

"I have to shower and get to the office. Will you be alright?"

"Yeah," I mumbled. I watched Liz cross back to the coffee pot to top off her mug.

"I'll try to talk to her," Liz said as she left the room.

"Don't!" I said, stopping Liz in her tracks. I was suddenly and irrationally panicked. What if Darcy was upset, I'd talked to Liz? What if she thought I was spreading rumors about what happened last night?

"What?" Liz looked at me like I was crazy, a moment away from laughing again.

"I don't ... don't tell her we talked about her."

"What is this? High school?"

"I just ... I don't want to make her uncomfortable. Like you said ... she's been through a lot this year. The last thing I want is to put any pressure on her."

"Alright," Liz said. "I won't bring anything up. Not unless she asks."

"Thank you." I sighed in relief.

"Try to relax today. You've been going nonstop."

"With the concert over, no one's expecting anything of me today," I told her, feeling the reality of this for the first time all morning. "I plan to rest!"

My phone buzzed on the table next to me, and I looked down to see Liam's name on the screen. Liam was the drummer of the Horizon, and one of my closest friends.

"I spoke too soon," I said, showing Liz the name on my screen. My sister knew my bandmates well, even having a brief relationship with my bass player at one point. I had disapproved of the relationship the whole time, and I was much relieved when Liz settled down with Eric, a high school English teacher.

"Good luck," Liz laughed. She left the room as I answered the phone.

"Hey man," I said, trying to keep the annoyance out of my voice.

"What's up?" Liam asked. "How was the concert last night?"

"Good. Fun to play in my hometown."

"Right. I bet."

"Everything good with you?"

"Yeah, man. Weird to have some time off."

"Uh-huh." I grumbled my agreement, though in reality I felt the opposite. I knew my bandmates were eager to continue our tour. They loved life on the road and the adventures they could have in each new city. I seemed to be the only one eager to find some stability in my life.

"Hey, I saw some of the new music you played. Where have you been hiding those songs, man?"

I felt my body go cold.

"You saw the concert?"

"Yeah. Some clips on YouTube. Those songs are killer, man! I showed them to the guys. With the right beat and some backup vocals, we might have our next album on our hands."

Panic was setting in, making my thoughts race. That music was *mine*. I hadn't written those songs for the Horizon.

"I don't know," I said, struggling for the right words. "I think they're better in the acoustic version. Sort of a solo thing, you know?"

"Solo?" Liam asked. I could almost feel him bristling on the other end of the phone. "What does *that* mean?"

"It was just something I was trying, man." I said, attempting to lessen the impact of those new songs. I wasn't ready to tell my bandmates that I wanted to branch out on my own for a bit. Right now, it was still an idea I was considering. "I had this concert on the books. And I knew it was a solo event. So, I just wanted to try out an acoustic sound."

"Got it," Liam said, but I could hear a tightness in his voice. "Well, the songs are good, man. If you want to keep working on them, we could really make 'em great."

I swallowed hard, ignoring Liam's dig. My bandmates always thought I couldn't do my thing without them. Was Liam saying I couldn't succeed on my own?

"Maybe you can find some time to write more while you're out there relaxing. You know, something other than this new *acoustic sound*."

"Hey, I have to go," I said, needing to get off the phone. "I'll talk to you later."

"Yeah, man. Talk to you soon."

I hung up and dropped my phone face down on the table. I never thought my bandmates would see that concert. How could something leak from my small hometown theater? I'd seen it as the perfect, *private* place to debut some new music with no risk, far away from the eyes of the world.

Curious, I picked up my phone and flipped to YouTube with a sense of dread in my stomach. I typed in a few key search terms, praying I wouldn't find anything. But there, right up top, I saw a still shot of my face at a microphone, the curtains of the Maplewood theater behind me. I clicked on the link and heard my own voice filter out from the phone's speakers. Under the video I saw a number rising in front of my eyes: 60.7 thousand views.

I needed some air. I pushed my way out of the house with my head swimming. Somehow, without realizing it, it seemed I had just launched my solo career.

9

DARCY

"Your usual?" Stephen asked from behind the counter.

"Yes, please. It's busy in here today!" I looked around the coffee shop to see most of the tables occupied. The store had opened only a few months ago, but it was quickly becoming one of the most popular spots in town.

"I know," Stephen said, a twinkle in his eye. Stephen and his wife Maura were recent transplants to Maplewood. They came here for a slower life, but I found it amusing that they brought the busy coffee shop with them. The place was reminiscent of some cafes I visited when I was on vacation in larger cities.

"Hey Darcy!" Maura came out from the back, bags of coffee in her hands. "Were you at the concert last night?"

I felt a blush creep into my cheeks. Why did the mere mention of Callum's concert turn me red?

"Yeah," I said, trying to keep my voice neutral.

"Wasn't it great? I can't believe we witnessed his new music! Who knew he would use the concert to announce a solo career!"

"What?" I asked. I didn't remember Callum mentioning anything to the crowd about officially branching out on his own. Had I missed something? It seemed unlikely given how drawn I was to Callum up on that stage. I had stared at him, hanging on every word from the privacy of the crowd.

"It's all over the Internet," Stephen said as he steamed milk for my latte. He made his voice serious and announcer-like as he said, "Callum Jones breaks away from the Horizon!"

"The video already has like a million views on YouTube."

"Did he really announce that?" I asked, still running through the concert in my head. I knew he premiered some new music, but he never talked about leaving his band.

"It was sort of *implied*, wasn't it?" Maura asked. "Callum Jones books a show in his hometown without his band? And then premieres a whole bunch of new music? Just him and his guitar! It was pretty magical."

Yes, the concert had been magical. And the events after the concert had been pretty exciting as well ... I pushed images of Callum's dressing room aside. As much as I had enjoyed it, I wouldn't let it happen again. Callum wasn't here for long. And if he really *was* breaking out on his own, he would soon be busy with TV appearances and interviews all over the country.

"I didn't know it was such a big deal," I said, taking the cup Stephen handed to me.

"Oh yeah," he said. "The world's going crazy over it. It's a whole new era for Callum Jones!"

"Speaking of!" Maura squealed, sending her eyes to the door of the cafe. I turned to see the very man they had been talking about waltzing through the door.

"Look who it is!" Stephen said as customers at the cafe

looked up. I saw people whispering to each other and Callum's name buzzed around the room.

"Welcome to The Cozy Mug!" Stephen called out, and Callum's eyes darted to the counter where they instantly locked with mine.

"Hey there," I said. There was no way to avoid an interaction. Unless I wanted to run behind the counter and hope for a back door, I was stuck in the small space with him.

"Darcy," he said. He sounded surprised, and maybe a bit nervous to find me here.

"What can I get you?" Stephen asked eagerly.

Maura elbowed him in the side.

"Relax," she whispered, though Callum and I could hear them. "We don't need to scare away the only celebrity who's come through those doors."

"Just a coffee," Callum told them, smiling. He turned back to me. "I was out for a walk. When I saw the cafe, I figured a bit more caffeine could serve me well."

It was like he was apologizing, trying to make it clear he hadn't come here to seek me out.

"Not much sleep?" I asked, but all at once I realized my mistake. I knew this question would send Callum's mind directly back to our time in the dressing room last night, as it did for me. I had been eager to make casual conversation, hoping to maintain distance between us. Instead, images of Callum standing naked in front of me now flooded into my head.

"You could say that," Callum said, his eyes dark as they scanned my face. I looked away. I needed to get out of there. I couldn't stand in front of him, thinking of all the ways he had touched me last night. It would only make me want more.

"Here you go." Stephen handed Callum's coffee across the table. When Callum tried to pay, Maura stepped in.

"It's on the house!" she said. She scanned the customers at the tables, many of them with phones carefully posed in Callum's direction. "The publicity's bound to bring us some business!"

I didn't miss the slight wince on Callum's face, the way his shoulders dropped. Was he upset about the attention? For someone with so many pictures on the Internet, I didn't expect him to be shy.

"You should tell them to tag the place in their posts," Callum said.

He looked back at me as I eyed the door, desperate to excuse myself.

"Can I talk to you?" he asked.

I wanted to say no. If we had been alone, I might have. But Maura and Stephen were watching us, listening to every word. I couldn't start any town rumors that I was rude to the great Callum Jones.

"Alright," I said.

"Outside?" I caught the way Callum's eyes scanned the room again, very aware of the attention his presence was getting.

I nodded and made my way to the door. I saw Callum drop money in the tip jar on the counter before he followed me out. Without speaking, I crossed the street to the park. Callum didn't seem in the mood to run into many people today, and I knew the park would be quiet at this mid-morning hour.

"Sounds like there's a lot of buzz about you this morning," I mused.

"So I saw," he said. I heard a frustration and darkness in his voice that was counter to the reaction I expected.

"You're not happy?" I asked. I sipped my latte as I led Callum down the walking path that circled the park.

"Believe it or not, I wasn't trying to make any sort of announcement last night. Kind of sucks when the whole world decides what you're trying to say without consulting you ..."

This was surprising. Callum seemed genuinely upset by whatever was being said about him online this morning. It made me glad for my small life in a small town where no one much cared what I was doing with my life.

"Sorry," Callum said, running his hand through his hair. "That's not what I came to talk to you about."

I braced myself. I had tried to make it clear to Callum that I understood last night was a onetime thing. I didn't need some sad story about his life on the road and how it wasn't the right time to settle down.

"It's alright," I said. "We don't have to talk about it."

"You didn't have to run out of there," Callum said. "I mean ... you could have stayed."

"It's alright," I said again. "It was late. And I had work ..."

I realized the irony of this statement as I walked in the park and sipped coffee at ten a.m. Clearly work wasn't that important if I was here right now.

"I didn't ..." he seemed conflicted, as if he wasn't sure what to say. "I'm sorry if things moved too fast last night."

"Don't worry about it." I felt like a broken record, saying the same words over and over. I felt trapped in a conversation I didn't want to have. It was time to make Callum understand I was fine with the way things happened last night. Otherwise, Callum and I were in for a very awkward summer.

"Look," I said, ready to lay it all on the line. "I don't regret what happened. I *wanted* it to happen. But I don't expect anything. I know you have a busy life. I do too! I have a business to worry about."

"I know that," Callum said.

"I'm focusing on the real estate office right now. I want to put my energy where it really matters, you know? So, let's just leave it. It was good that it happened, but it doesn't have to happen again, okay?"

My heart beat hard in my chest, but a sense of relief washed over me. There, I had said it. And now there would be no confusion about what I expected. I wasn't some clingy fan who would send him love letters and ask when I would see him again. I was an adult who could make adult decisions, and Callum was free to make his.

"Okay," Callum said. "I get it." I sensed hesitation in his voice, and that same sadness that had hung over him from the moment I saw him today. I couldn't help wondering if it was part of some well-rehearsed, moody-musician vibe.

"I have to get to work," I said, unsure what else he wanted me to say. From this part of the park, I could easily cut through to my office which was just down the road on Main Street.

"Come to dinner with me."

The words stopped me in my tracks. I turned to look at him and saw a slight smile turning up one corner of his mouth.

"I can't," I said, searching his face. Was he joking with me? "Like I said—I'm focusing on my business right now."

With that, I walked away, leaving Callum standing on the path. I felt a sense of accomplishment and pride over how I had handled things with him. Last night was fun, but now I had released Callum from any obligation to me. Yes, it felt good. And that feeling was almost enough to mask the hurt and sadness I felt as I walked away from Callum Jones.

10

CALLUM

I *want to put my energy where it really matters, you know?*

I sighed as Darcy's words played over and over in my head. My coffee had long gone cold, but I still walked the park, fighting my way through my thoughts. How could so much have gone wrong in one night?

When I first kissed Darcy, I didn't understand what a hold that kiss (and everything that came after) would have on me. Sure, I had always found her smart and beautiful. But the feelings coursing through me now were more than some crush. I wanted to be near her, and Darcy's efforts to push me away left me feeling confused and wounded.

And on top of these personal problems, I was facing furious bandmates and an irate manager who thought I had somehow gone behind all their backs to break up the band. I had spent the morning on the phone, trying to make them understand that my concert last night hadn't been some big statement. I only wanted to try out some new music in a safe place.

Needless to say, the band and Brady were not convinced.

And even worse, every time I checked the YouTube clip,

the number of views had jumped up. And my name was officially trending. News outlets or reporters filled my voicemail, asking for a statement. So far I was ignoring them, but I knew it was only a matter of time before I would need to give a response. I took out my phone to see if I could report the video to YouTube. Maybe I could claim a copyright infringement and ask them to take it down. But my mind started floating to all the strange outcomes that might come from this.

I imagined the headlines: "Rock star silences his fans" or "Famous singer advocates censorship." I hated I even had to think this way, but I had been in the public eye long enough to know that anything could be used against me. No, I would need to make a statement. It was the only way to clear up this mess.

I pulled up my email and sent off a quick message to my publicist:

Hey Andrea,

Can you draft a statement for me? The music last night wasn't meant to be an announcement of any solo career. It was just me playing around with some new music in what I thought was a safe space. Would love a statement to send to all these people requesting interviews.

Thanks,

Callum

There—one problem down. I knew Andrea would create something to fend off the hungry sharks of the media. At least for a little while. I sighed. I had never been so glad to have a media team that could handle things like this!

With this problem on the way to being solved, my

worries about Darcy floated back to the surface. Had I given her the impression I didn't want something serious? It was possible. After all, if Liz had asked me just a few months ago if I wanted to find a relationship this summer, I would have laughed in her face. But lately, I had been feeling the urge to settle down. And the presence of Darcy wouldn't leave my mind.

Year after year, relationship after relationship, Darcy was the girl I had never stopped thinking about. In my last year of high school, only weeks before heading off to college, I had thought we might finally have our chance. I took Darcy on a date, beaming the entire time to have her on my arm. But it hadn't worked out. Darcy had shown me she wasn't interested in me in that way.

Just like now, I told myself. Darcy was making it clear she saw last night as a one-off event. She didn't want anything more with me. But did Darcy really know me? Sure, she knew the rock star she saw in magazines, a carefully curated image my media team perpetuated. But would she feel the same way if she knew the real Callum Jones?

I threw my coffee cup in the trash with renewed energy. I could get to know Darcy and, in turn, she would get to know me. Darcy would see that I wasn't the person she thought I was. And then, if she still wanted nothing to do with me, I could walk away. At least I would have given it my best shot.

Feeling more energized than I had all morning, I left the park and took off down Main Street until I reached my destination. With a slight smirk, I pushed through the door of Dream Home Realty.

"What are you doing here?" Liz asked. She sat at her desk with a pen in her mouth, flipping through a folder of papers.

"Alright, we got the contract." Darcy emerged from the copy room, looking down at the contract in her hands.

"We have a visitor!" Liz announced.

I saw Darcy flip into realtor mode, a huge smile on her face as she prepared to welcome a new client. But then she saw me standing in the doorway. I tried not to feel insulted as the smile dropped quickly from her face.

"What are you doing here?" Darcy asked. It was curt and cold, a clear indication she was not happy to see me.

"*Wow*, Darcy," Liz said, responding to the harshness in her friend's tone. "Can't the man come by to say hi to his sister?"

I watched Darcy relax her face. At least she wasn't scowling at me anymore.

"Sorry," she muttered. Darcy crossed to her desk and kept her eyes on the paperwork in front of her. It seemed she was resigned to ignore me.

"Who knew your concert would make such a stir?" Liz said as I took a seat in one of the chairs set up across from her desk. I dropped with a groan when I heard her words.

"Don't remind me," I said. "This whole thing is getting blown way out of proportion."

"Might be a good time to capitalize," Liz said. "Seems like all your fans are ecstatic over the idea!"

"I'm not sure my bandmates are so excited."

"Yeah, but they'll get over it. Haven't you been thinking about going out on your own?"

"Sure," I said. "But not in any serious way. It's just something I like to daydream about."

I let my eyes slide over to Darcy's desk, wondering if she was listening to us. I secretly hoped she was. Anything to let Darcy see the real me.

"So, look," I said, standing up and making a slow cross to

Darcy's desk, hoping to draw her attention. I was pleased to see her look up at me, her eyebrows raised.

"I've been thinking about some property."

"Really?!" I heard Liz squeal from the other side of the room. I inwardly groaned at my sister. I needed her to be quiet right now. This conversation was meant for Darcy, and Liz's interjections would only complicate it.

"Property?" Darcy asked.

"Right." I kept my eyes on her. "I want to see what's available."

"You're thinking of moving back?" Liz asked. She was standing now, moving around to the side of her desk so she could perch on it. Though I answered Liz's question, I kept my eyes pinned on Darcy.

"I'm thinking more of a commercial property. Something I could turn into a business."

"A business?" Good, I had caught Darcy's attention. I held back a smirk as I congratulated myself on drawing her into conversation.

"A recording studio," I told her. "Liz is always complaining about how I don't visit enough. If we had a recording studio in town, I could come here anytime I need to record music."

Darcy seemed skeptical, as if trying to figure out if I was telling the truth.

"You won't find any recording studios in Maplewood. Not in any of the surrounding towns, either."

"That's alright. I can renovate it. Some of the most famous studios were converted from other spaces. Could be a cool project. And it might even bring some other artists to town."

"How exciting!" Liz said. "There are plenty of spots you could look at. A bunch of old factories and stores shut down ages ago and the owners don't know what to do with them. We can look at some this afternoon—"

"I want Darcy to take me."

This silenced Liz, and I watched my sister look between Darcy and myself. Slowly, she seemed to understand that something else was going on here. To Darcy's credit, she didn't seem shocked by my words. She only looked at me casually before dropping her eyes, still pretending that the contract on her desk required all of her attention.

"Liz usually handles our commercial buildings," she said, dismissing me. I had no way of knowing if this was true, but I wouldn't let it deter me.

"I'd like *you*."

She looked up and stared at me, her gaze full of challenge and a hint of anger. I stared back, unwilling to back down. I needed Darcy to know who I was as a person, and if forcing her to show me real estate properties was the only way to do this, then so be it.

"No," Darcy said.

It was a simple and decisive answer. I hadn't expected an outright decline, but I wasn't ready to give up.

"You wouldn't turn down business, would you?" I asked. "Not when I have good money to spend." I saw the hesitation on Darcy's face. It would be impossible for her not to think about all that rock-star money sitting somewhere in my bank account. I knew Darcy was looking to expand into the next town, and I knew an all-cash offer from me might just seal the deal.

"Have Liz take you," Darcy tried again. Her voice was conflicted, and I could tell she was losing steam. Still, I didn't want to push my luck. If I was determined to show her I was a nice, down-to-earth guy, then I needed to start now.

"Look," I said, getting closer to her so our conversation

could be more private. "It's just looking at some properties. It's nothing more than that. And I love Liz, but if I take her along, she'll spend the whole time trying to make my decision for me."

"I can hear you," Liz called out, and I glanced over to give her a rueful smile.

"I need someone objective," I said, returning to Darcy. When I caught her gaze, I saw something shift there, a gentleness that was more in line with the Darcy I knew last night. The Darcy I held in my arms ...

She stared back, and I saw the hint of hunger in her eyes.

"Fine," she said. She stood up from her desk with a sigh. I watched as she carried the contract over to Liz's desk.

"Deal with this," she told Liz. She crossed back to her desk and grabbed her purse before opening her desk drawer to sort through what looked like dozens of keys. I watched her pick out the ones she wanted, dropping them one by one into her bag.

"Come on," she said. Darcy squeezed her way through desks and chairs as she headed for the front door.

"Where?" I asked.

"You want to see properties, don't you?"

Now it was my turn to be surprised.

"You want to go *now*?"

"Do you have something better to do?" Darcy asked. I smiled at her and shook my head.

No, I did not. Right now, there was nothing more important than spending time with Darcy and showing her exactly what sort of a person I was.

11

DARCY

"As you can see, it gets good light in the afternoons."

I watched as Callum walked around the large, open warehouse. He observed the windows and nodded at my comments. He spun around, and I saw him imagining different furniture pieces in the room or where he could put walls. Was he really serious about this recording studio thing?

"The ceiling is really high," he said. "It would be difficult to soundproof the place."

"It would," I agreed, though in truth I didn't know anything about recording studios and what the space might look like. Liz and I primarily stuck with residential properties but, in a small town like ours, it wasn't uncommon for us to list some of the commercial buildings for friends or family.

"The last place was closer to the downtown area. That might be helpful for a new business."

"It might ..." I said, still trying to understand what he

was looking for, "if you're hoping for a lot of foot traffic ... is that the sort of thing you need for a recording studio?"

He seemed to really consider the question as he looked back at me.

"I guess you're right," he said. It surprised me to realize he might be taking my advice seriously. "Somewhere a bit further from Main Street might be helpful. Quieter. We might be recording late into the night, so we wouldn't want to disturb anyone with all the coming and going."

Callum walked toward the back where there were a few offices along the wall. This place used to be a newspaper office, with a big open space for reporter desks and a few private spaces in the back. The local paper had downsized quite a bit in the last few years, with most reporters working remotely, and they no longer needed such a big space.

"You do realize that Maplewood isn't exactly crawling with musicians?" I asked. Callum was inside one of the offices, opening and closing the blinds on the windows that looked out onto the main room.

"Oh, it won't be locals coming here," he said. "It'll be other artists I know."

"And *why* would they come to Maplewood?" I asked. I liked our town, but it definitely wasn't a tourist destination. It was a sleepy place where all the restaurants closed by nine p.m. I couldn't imagine famous rock stars flocking to the town to record their next album.

"People are looking for an escape," Callum told me. I had a feeling he was speaking from experience. "They want somewhere quiet where they can focus on the music. They're going to spend ten or twelve hours in the studio. Where they sleep isn't very important."

We walked back to the open room, and I shifted on my

feet, waiting for his opinion of the fourth property of the day.

"What do you think?" I asked. I was itching to get out of the place after an afternoon with Callum. He kept looking at me with an intense stare that made me instantly flash back to the previous night in his dressing room. I needed to drive back to the office and excuse myself to get back to work.

"It's not right," he sighed. "It doesn't have the right vibe. Too cold."

"Got it," I said, holding my tongue. Every place we visited had some "vibe" problem. It was too clinical or too cold. One of the properties was too "spiritual", whatever that meant!

"Let's find another," he said, and I inwardly groaned.

"That's pretty much it," I told him. "I've shown you what we have available in the Maplewood area. Anything else, we'll have to go much further out."

"No problem," he said, smiling as he crossed to the door. "I've got all day."

I felt anxiety and annoyance flood my chest.

"Callum!" I cried, finally letting my frustration out. He spun around, a slight smile on his face. "*I* don't have all day. I have to get back to the office."

He crossed closer and gave me that stare again. I was suddenly on his dressing room counter, feeling his mouth on me, eager for more. I shook my head and forced the image out of my mind.

"Blow off work," he said, his voice low. "We could just enjoy ourselves."

His eyes fell down to my lips, and I thought he might kiss me. I wasn't about to let that happen. Last night was a onetime thing, and I couldn't let it become a pattern. Not when I knew he was only here for the summer. If I got too attached, I would be the one hurt when he left. I reminded myself of our date all those years ago, when he had no problem leaving without a word.

"I can't," I said, pushing past him and heading for the door. I didn't stop. I simply set my sights on the car outside and made a beeline for it. He followed me and I locked the building up in silence. I was relieved that he stayed quiet while we returned to the car and had a silent drive back to the real estate office.

\#

"Thanks for showing me around," he said, getting out of the car. He finally seemed to realize that I wasn't interested in spending my time with him. At least, I hoped he was realizing that. All this time together was affecting me in ways I didn't like. I couldn't stop thinking about what would happen if I just let him kiss me. If I just gave in to him one more time ...

The slam of the car door pulled me out of these thoughts, and I looked back at him.

"Thanks," I said, but his confused face made me realize I had misspoken. "I mean, you're welcome."

"Hey Darcy!" The voice gave me a jolt of instant panic. I turned to see John, my ex-fiancé, walking toward me, grocery bags in hand.

"John," I said as I breathed through a tightness in my chest. I hadn't spoken to him in months. I had been so relieved when all the wedding business was concluded, and we didn't have to endure strained phone calls and awkward meetings. After the final details of returning rings and getting addresses for his relatives who had sent engagement presents, I hoped we wouldn't see each other again. Of course, I knew that was unrealistic. We lived in Maplewood, after all.

"I haven't seen you in a while," he said. His T-shirt was too tight, showing off the hard-earned muscles of his arms and his chest. It used to be enticing to me, but now I couldn't see anything except a man far too full of himself to care about anyone else.

"Hey, man." Callum stepped forward, putting himself between me and John. My eyes flipped over to the office door, hoping Liz might notice what was happening and come out to save me.

"Callum," John said. John had gone to high school with all of us, so the two men knew each other a bit. Since Callum was older, their paths wouldn't have crossed much, and I didn't know what Callum knew about my past relationship with John.

"What's going on, man?" I couldn't miss the hint of threat in Callum's voice. It made me wonder if he knew quite a bit about my history with John. Had Liz talked to him about it?

"I saw you were in town," John said, flicking his eyes between me and Callum. "Sorry I couldn't make the show."

"No worries, man." The words they used were friendly, but there was a darkness underneath them. I could sense tension building between them, an unspoken challenge that I didn't know how to diffuse.

"So, what are you two up to?" John asked. He had likely watched us get out of the car together. I remembered that possessiveness he had when we were together, always suspicious of other men I was talking to.

"I was just showing Callum some properties," I said, wanting to assure John that everything here was professional. But Callum spoke at the same time, talking over me.

"I don't think that's any concern of yours, man," Callum said. "Not anymore, anyway."

Yes, he clearly knew my history with John. And from the looks of things, he wasn't thrilled about it.

"Whoa, man," John said. He put the brown paper grocery bag on the trunk of my car, and I felt my stomach drop. The two men were squaring off against each other, clearly sizing each other up as they shared tense words. "I wasn't talking to you."

"If you're talking to Darcy, you're talking to me," Callum said. He stepped forward and John and Callum were face to face, their chests puffed up as they glared at each other.

"Knock it off," I said, shaking my head. "Callum, let's go inside."

Callum took another second to scowl at John before sliding his eyes to where I stood next to him. With a slight laugh in John's direction, meant to belittle him, he turned and followed me back toward the door of the office.

"You're gonna let a girl tell you what to do?" John asked. Suddenly, Callum was back in John's face and then, before we realized what was happening, he shoved him.

"Enough!" I yelled, but John was shoving back, and I knew a full-blown fight was minutes away from happening.

"I'm leaving," I cried out. I rushed back to the driver's side of the car and got in, slamming the door hard behind me. I refused to look in my rear-view mirror, afraid of what I might see there. I simply slammed the gas pedal and sped out of there as John's bag of groceries flew off the trunk and scattered all over the pavement.

12

CALLUM

"What were you thinking?" I sat in Liz's kitchen, a towel full of ice pressed to my eye. "What did you expect me to do?" I asked. "He was in my face!"

"Walk away! Do you think getting into a fist fight with Darcy's ex is going to make her like you more?"

"He was being an ass," I cried out. My head was throbbing from where John had clocked me hard in the eye. Luckily, I got a few good punches in before Liz heard the commotion and put herself between us to break up the fight.

"You deal with assholes all the time," Liz said. She sat down next to me at the table. "Thank God no one saw you. It would *not* be a good look to have this plastered all over the Internet."

It had all happened so quickly I hadn't had time to consider that. I sighed as I realized Liz was right—I needed to keep my cool. That sort of bad publicity could kill a career. I leaned back against the chair, feeling the adrenaline finally draining out of me. Liz had bundled me into the car as soon as John stormed away, yelling back curses as he did so. I told her not to worry about me, that she should get back to work, but she locked up the real estate office and took me home.

"I shouldn't have done it," I said, finally ready to admit I had overreacted. "But all that stuff you told me about him. About how he treated Darcy. I couldn't think of anything except making him pay."

"Darcy doesn't need you to fight her battles for her. She gave the guy a piece of her mind when she left."

"I know. God, she's probably so mad at me." I brought the ice away from my eye and rested my elbows on the kitchen table. It was stupid to fight John like that. Darcy had tried to stop us, but I didn't listen to her. Now she was probably furious with me, angry I had made some show of defending her when we weren't even together. I had completely overreacted and embarrassed her in the process.

"I'm sure she'll get over it," Liz said. "She'll probably be mad she wasn't there to see that punch to John's mouth."

I smirked a bit and remembered the satisfaction I felt when I got that swing in. I certainly didn't enjoy violence, and I wasn't in the habit of getting into fights. But if anyone deserved a good sock in the mouth, it sounded like this guy did.

"I should apologize," I said. I didn't want to sit here all night with the guilt I felt churning in my stomach.

"Maybe you should give her a day to cool off," Liz said. She glanced at the purple bruise forming around my eye. "And to let that heal."

"It's only going to look worse tomorrow," I mumbled.

"Don't you dare tell Alan you got in a fight!" Liz said, referencing my nephew. "The last thing I need is him thinking fighting is *cool* because his uncle is doing it."

"What do you suggest?" I asked, laughing.

"Tell him you were playing catch and got a baseball to the eye." I rolled my eyes at her, sure he wouldn't believe it, but Liz doubled down. "He's five! Whatever you say he'll believe."

I stood up from the table but had to grab the back of the chair when I did so. I felt a rush of dizziness that made me squeeze my eyes closed, sending pain through my face from the bruise.

"Are you sure you should go?" Liz asked, but I quickly recovered.

"I'm alright," I said. "Any idea where I might find Darcy?"

Liz looked at me, as if debating whether she should tell me. If she had her way, I would stay home and rest. But I think she knew I wasn't going to do that. If she didn't tell me where Darcy was, I would simply drive around, trying a few likely spots to see if I could find her.

Finally, Liz sighed.

"We've been texting," she said. "When she knew the office was clear, she went back to catch up on work."

It was almost six at this point, but I knew Darcy was the type to work as long as it took. And I had taken up her entire afternoon making her show me properties. I suddenly felt guilty, knowing Darcy would be at the office late because of me.

"Think she'll still be there in half an hour?" I asked, an idea forming.

"For sure," Liz said. "Another offer came in for the hardware store, so she'll review it. I'm not sure why she bothers, though. She's just going to deny it."

"A bad offer?" I asked.

"Not bad at all," Liz said, shaking her head. "It's pretty

close to asking, which is saying a lot since it's already listed too high. But none of the offers are ever good enough for Darcy. That place is really special to her, you know? It's hard to put a price on something with so many memories."

I nodded, remembering my most recent visit to the hardware store. Darcy took good care of the place, and it was easy to see how much she loved it. I understood why she wanted a good paycheck for something so special to her.

"Tell the kids I'm sorry to miss dinner," I said. I grabbed my keys and headed out to the driveway, thinking of what I would say to make Darcy forgive me.

#

"I know I'm the last person you want to see right now," I said when Darcy came to the door. A steady rain was falling outside, and I pulled the hood of my jacket over my head in an attempt to stay dry. Darcy had locked the front door since it was after five o'clock, but I saw her sitting at her desk through the glass. I knocked gently, not wanting to startle her, and she came over to unlock the door.

"I see things escalated," Darcy said, sweeping her eyes up to the angry bruise that had formed around my eye.

"He looks worse," I said, smiling at her. She smiled back, accepting my joke, but she didn't make a move to open the door any further or invite me in. The rain fell around me, and I worried about the food in my hand getting wet.

"I brought a peace offering," I said. I held up the plastic bag in my hand. "I figured you haven't had dinner yet. Could we talk?"

She looked at me, trying to decide, but then she opened the door fully to let me inside, saving me from the rain.

"I won't be long," I said. I set the food on Liz's desk and took off my jacket that was dripping with water as I hung it on the coat rack. I took the seat at Liz's desk while Darcy sat back at her own. "I only want to apologize."

She looked back at me, but there was no hint of anger or frustration in her eyes. She seemed willing to let me talk, and so I launched into the speech I had been formulating the full ride over here.

"I shouldn't have let him get to me," I said. "I'm sorry I let him pull me into a stupid fight. And I'm sorry if it seemed like I didn't think you could fight your own battles or anything like that. I wasn't trying to embarrass you."

"I don't need you to defend me," Darcy said, her voice even. "It's not like we're together or anything like that."

The words hit me in the gut, but I tried to keep my face neutral. Darcy had made it very clear that she wasn't interested in a relationship. I knew that, so I shouldn't be surprised or hurt when she reinforced it.

"I know we're not," I said. "But I still don't want some ass mistreating you. I'd do the same thing for Liz, you know?"

It was hard to read her expression as she watched me. She seemed subdued, as if she couldn't quite figure out what she wanted to say. But I took it as a win that she was at least letting me have a conversation and wasn't telling me to leave.

"You got a few good punches in?" Darcy asked, and I delighted in the small smile on her face. Once again, I felt the satisfaction of that hit to John's mouth.

"It would have been worse if Liz hadn't broken us up," I said.

"He *is* an ass," she said, and I felt the tension break between us. "I kind of wish I had been there to see it."

"Liz can tell you all about it," I smiled. We were quiet then, both unsure of what to say next. I saw the papers still strewn on her desk and knew she probably had more work she wanted to finish up. I didn't want to make her night any longer than I already had.

"Anyway," I said, standing up. "I'll let you finish your work. I hope Chinese food is alright." I gestured to the bag that was sitting on the desk. "Liz said it's your usual meal for working late."

"It is," Darcy said. She smiled at me, and I felt a warmth in my chest. It felt good to do something nice for her, and it made me thrilled to know I had done something to make her happy.

I grabbed my still-dripping coat from the coat rack and slid into it. The sound of rain surrounded the building and filled the silence around us.

"Could you do me a favor?" Darcy asked. I spun around to see her close to me, leaning against Liz's desk.

"Of course," I said. "But if you want me to beat someone else up, it might have to wait until tomorrow."

Darcy rolled her eyes at me, and we smiled. I was hopeful this meant our friendship had been restored and we could put today's incident behind us. I could only hope I wouldn't run into John anytime soon.

"I walked over here from my house," Darcy said. I saw her eyes slide to the front door where we watched the rain falling steadily. "Would you mind dropping me off?"

"No problem," I said.

"It's only a few blocks," she said, as if wanting to assure me it wouldn't take up too much time. "I just didn't know it was going to rain. If I can avoid getting soaked to the skin, I'd certainly like to."

The image of Darcy in the rain, her clothes wet, brought a sudden flash of desire. I pushed it away, forcing myself back to the present.

"Of course," I said. "Do you need to finish anything up here?"

"All done," Darcy said. "I don't think I can focus on anything else for the night."

I handed her a sweater from the coat rack, which I assumed was hers, and she thanked me for it. She gathered the rest of her things, and we rushed out to the car shielding ourselves from the heavy raindrops falling around us.

13

DARCY

We drove the short distance back to my house, the smell of fried food wafting through the car. My stomach grumbled at the smell, and I realized how hungry I was. I was touched Callum had brought it for me and surprised by the kindness of the gesture. I never expected him to apologize for his fight with John.

"Up here on the right," I said, pointing out my small Cape Cod-style cottage. Even in the pouring rain the house was quaint. I always felt better coming home to it, and I was proud of the way I had fixed it up, bringing it back to its former glory.

Callum slowed the car to park along the sidewalk.

"How nice," he said, smiling at me. I thought about the pouring rain and the bag of food sitting at my feet. From the size of the bag, it looked like far too much food for one person. And Callum had been so sweet tonight ...

"Have you eaten?" I asked. I waited for his reply as the windshield wipers squeaked against the windshield.

"Not yet," he admitted. "Liz probably saved a plate for me."

"It looks like I have plenty for two," I said carefully. "Do you want to come in?"

It was only hours ago that I was telling myself to keep my distance from Callum and not to let myself get too attached. But the rain falling around us as everything got dark outside made the rest of the world fall away. I wanted a quiet dinner where I could enjoy someone else's company.

"If you're up for it," he said. "I'd love to."

The rain was falling harder, and neither of us had an umbrella. I hadn't brought anything except a sweater when I walked back to the office. Callum took the food, and we made a run for it back to the house, the rain beating onto our heads and shoulders. I cried out as I struggled to fit my key into the lock and Callum tried to shield us both with his jacket, standing close to me. Finally, the key turned, and I pushed inside, both of us laughing and dripping from the downpour. I looked up at him as he ran his hands through his hair, flicking water out of it.

"Food might be a little soggy," he laughed. I smiled back at him and told him it was alright as I peeled my soaked sweater off and hung it by the front door.

Since Callum had a coat on, he was less wet than I was, and I was glad to see his shirt was mostly dry when he took it off. But his curly dark hair was wet, dripping down around his eyes in a way that made him even more handsome than usual.

"I'm going to change," I said, feeling a slight shiver as I peeled my eyes away from him. "The kitchen is just off to the right."

Callum nodded, and I rushed upstairs to take off my soaked jeans and T-shirt. I agonized over what I should put on, longing for sweatpants but not wanting to look too casual with Callum setting up food in my kitchen. But it had been a long day and ultimately comfort won out. I picked out my favorite sweatpants, an old pair with "Maplewood High" in block letters up the leg, thinking Callum might get a kick out of them. Along with a plain, loose-fitting T-shirt and a zip-up sweatshirt to ward off the chill from the rain.

I couldn't help checking my hair and makeup in the vanity mirror. Using a brush, I smoothed out the knots and was relieved to see my mascara hadn't run. Adding a touch of blush brought color back to my pale face. At the last minute I added a swipe of lip gloss as well before I rushed down the stairs, hoping I hadn't taken too long.

"If you need it ..." I said, tossing a towel toward Callum. He had laid out the food on my small kitchen table and was busy setting plates and silverware out.

"Hope it's okay I looked around," he said, nodding down to the table he was setting.

"Of course. I'm just glad I did the dishes this morning!" We smiled and Callum brought the towel to his hair, rubbing it against his curls. I went to the fridge where I stood on tiptoes to grab my emergency bottle of wine, usually up there for particularly stressful days at the office.

"Is red alright?" I asked. Callum nodded, and I grabbed two stemless wine glasses from the cabinet. For a few minutes the space was filled with the pop of the bottle and the clink of silverware as we set up for the meal in front of us. Something about it felt natural and calm, as if we had done this sort of thing many times before.

I poured us each a glass of wine and we sat down.

"Thanks again for this," I said as we each took a good sip of wine and settled into the food. "If it wasn't for this, I'd probably be sitting down to a bowl of cereal or something."

I hadn't intended for this to sound sad, but I suddenly felt embarrassed as the words came out of my mouth. When my dad got sick, cooking was one of the first things that went out the window. We often resorted to takeout or quick microwave meals that didn't require endless cleanup. On nights I spent with John, he would usually cook. His dietary specifications were detailed and after a few failed attempts on my part to cook dinner for us, I gave up and let him take the lead on whatever he wanted to cook.

"You and me both," Callum laughed, and I felt better. "Thank God I'm staying with Liz this summer, or I would probably starve. I'm *way* too used to catered meals and room service. I think I'd burn the house down if I tried to turn on the stove."

"Not much of a cook?" I asked. I was eating enthusiastically, realizing just how hungry I was. The food had grown slightly cold, but we didn't mind. We were both simply glad to be inside a warm house and filling our stomachs.

"I never learned," Callum shrugged. "I went from living in a dorm room cooking ramen in the microwave to being on the road where food would simply appear in front of me."

"It must have been a big change," I said. I thought about myself as a college student and just how immature I was. I wasn't sure I would have been able to handle being launched to fame and suddenly traveling the world giving concerts.

"*Huge* change," Callum said, his eyes widening. "I was so focused on the music and putting out songs that people could connect to. I never really thought about everything else that came with people *hearing* those songs. The idea of people wanting to meet me or interview me for magazines was never something I ever thought about."

"Really?" I asked. "You always seemed so comfortable with it."

"No way!" he laughed. Callum refilled my wine glass and then topped off his own. "It makes me *so* uncomfortable. I only do it because it's part of the job. If we don't have fans, there's no one to listen to new music and no audience to sing to. I sign autographs and take pictures so I can keep writing and performing. That's what's important to me."

"I don't know if I could do it," I admitted. I stood up from the table to grab a glass of water and placed one in front of Callum as well. "Be in the public eye like that. I would be so nervous to make a mistake or say the wrong thing."

I thought back to the one time I was forced to participate in a school play. It must have been in the fourth grade when we performed a dramatized version of the signing of the Declaration of Independence. Two lines of narration kept me up at night for weeks, and I couldn't get off that stage fast enough!

"It's not easy," Callum admitted, and I heard a fatigue in his voice that made me sad. But then he chuckled, changing the mood. "Liz said I was lucky no one witnessed that fight earlier. I guess I should be glad no one in town's figured out the value of a good tabloid photo."

I groaned, imagining the newspaper article that would accompany something like that.

"Oh my God, that would have made things so much worse!" I laughed.

"As long as they list me as the winner, I'm alright with it," Callum laughed.

"Oh, is that the most important thing?" I asked, smirking at him. "To win the fight?"

"Of course. You can't fight over a woman and *lose*."

I blushed at Callum's open admission that he was

fighting for me. I knew I should reject the idea, but it made me feel warm and appreciated in a way I hadn't felt in a long time. I looked back at Callum, comfortable in the silence between us. I felt deliciously full and relaxed from the wine in front of us. The rain outside was a gentle sound that lulled me into calm, and Callum was looking at me with those warm brown eyes that made me feel seen.

"It's still coming down out there," I said, looking over to the window. "Maybe you should stay until it calms down a bit."

He seemed surprised by the words, but he quickly recovered.

"Makes sense," he said, playing along. "Better to be safe."

We cleaned up the food, finding moments of gentle touches between us as we passed containers of food into the fridge and dropped plates into the sink. I filled our wine glasses and guided Callum to the living room, the only other room on the first floor. My body felt tense with anticipation, wound up by the brush of his hand on my own and the closeness of his body behind me as we navigated the small kitchen. I knew Callum felt it too. He was looking at me with unbridled hunger, though I could tell he was waiting for my move.

I settled onto the couch, pulling my legs up to sit cross-legged where I could face him on the other side. My body felt warm and flushed, and I slid off the sweatshirt I wore. He settled across from me, watching me discard this top layer as he took a long sip from his wine glass. He placed the glass on the coffee table and turned back to me with a smirk.

"I didn't think I would be here tonight," he said. The honesty in his words surprised me, and I felt a flush of heat that went straight to my core. Those curls were still damp across his forehead, falling around his eyes, and I looked again at the red and purple bruise that surrounded his left eye. I knew I shouldn't condone his fighting, but I had never had someone fight for me like that, and I had to admit it stirred something inside of me.

"Does it hurt?" I asked. I let my hand wander up to his cheek, gently running a finger along his temple. I was careful not to touch the bruised skin of his eye.

"It does," he said, his voice low as his eyes searched my face. "Does it look bad?"

"I don't want you to hurt," I said, letting my finger run along the stubble around his chin. "But you look badass."

He let out a single laugh, and I could tell he enjoyed this. His eyes got darker. He lifted a hand up and suddenly his hand was on my breast, causing me to gasp as his fingers explored.

"So that's why you invited me over," he laughed. I couldn't take it any longer. His fingers pressed against the fabric of my T-shirt, sending a promise of things to come, and I wanted more. I leaned forward to put my hands on his thighs and pressed my mouth against his.

14

CALLUM

Her hands pressed into my thighs, dangerously close to the arousal that was already growing between my legs. Her mouth was warm, and I tasted wine on her tongue as she pressed against me, eager for more. My palm was on her breast, but the fabric of her T-shirt and bra wasn't giving me the access I needed.

Darcy seemed desperate for me, her mouth hard against mine, and I was shocked by how eager she seemed, how ready. Not that I should be surprised. We had spent the whole meal stealing glances at each other, both silently wondering what the night would bring. There was something so sexy about her dressed in sweatpants and a T-shirt, as if I had a glimpse of the true Darcy, not the professional facade she put on at the office.

And now she was across from me, practically begging me to give her more. And I wasn't about to disappoint her.

"Come upstairs," she said, and I felt my length press harder against my jeans.

"After you," I said. She stood up, and I instantly missed those hands on my thighs. But then I saw her heading for the stairs, and I followed close behind. I couldn't keep myself from reaching out to cup her butt through those sweatpants as she walked a few steps ahead of me. And I was delighted when she looked over her shoulder and smiled at me, clearly enjoying my attention.

Her room was small and neat, like the rest of the house, and it was only a few steps before we tumbled to the bed, Darcy pulling me on top of her. I found her mouth and pressed my hips against her, straining against my jeans. I wanted to feel more of her, and I stood up to pull those sweatpants off her, leaving her in her T-shirt and underwear —an adorable sight. She looked at me with anticipation as I brought my hands to my belt and slowly undid it. Suddenly she was off the bed, her hands at my waist, pushing my own hands away. She undid the button of my jeans and the zipper, her eyes on mine.

Then she pushed down my jeans, leaving me in my briefs just as I had done with her. I stepped out of the pants and felt Darcy's hand at the bulge of my underwear, stroking. I pushed her back toward the bed where we fell back again, my mouth on hers even as I pressed my hard-ness between her legs. Only thin layers of fabric stood between us, and I groaned as I felt how ready she was for me. Her hands moved up the back of my arms as I crushed my mouth into hers, pressing my tongue into her mouth. She yanked at my shirt, and I pulled it over my head and threw it to the floor.

"Roll over," Darcy whispered, and I couldn't obey fast enough, flipping over to my back. I thought she would straddle me, instead she kissed down my chest, and suddenly her mouth was lower, kissing down toward my length.

"God, yes," I groaned, looking down at her as I felt tightness build low in my stomach. She bit her bottom lip, a slight moment of hesitation, but then her fingers ran along the waistband of my shorts, and she freed me. There was a mischievous expression on her face as she took in what stood tall in front of her. A second later her tongue was warm and soft against me, and I groaned again, trying to keep myself still. I was rewarded with the warmth of her lips enveloping me, and I felt waves of pleasure as she pressed me deeper into her mouth.

It was all I could do not to push myself further into her. But I wanted Darcy to set the pace, and I forced myself to sit still while she began a gentle rhythm. I watched as she moved up and down, nearly holding my breath as she got deeper with each pass. Her tongue worked against me even as her lips squeezed tighter, and suddenly her hand was there too. I bit the inside of my mouth to keep from calling out as new sensations threatened to undo me.

"That's amazing," I said to her, and she picked up her pace. My eyes closed in the pleasure of it all, but then I felt a shock of pain as I squeezed my bruised eye too tightly. I must have jumped, because Darcy pulled away, a question in her eyes.

"Are you alright?" she asked. I was fixated on those pink and shiny lips, wanting them back where they had come from. But I didn't like that confusion in her eyes. And besides, I needed to feel more of her.

"Come here," I said. I pulled her arm to bring her face back up to my own and kissed her long and deep. My erection pressed against her stomach, and I brought my hand up beneath her shirt to finally push aside her bra and feel the hard nub of her nipple. She moaned into my mouth, and I felt her hand reach down to wrap around me. I circled her nipple with my finger, remembering how much she enjoyed it the last time we did this.

"Don't stop," Darcy begged, and I moved my hand to her other breast. My hips were pressing up, eager for more, and I felt Darcy rubbing herself against me. I watched small waves of pleasure pass through her as she teased herself with my length. She sat up on her knees, giving herself some distance, and then pulled her shirt over her head. I was delighted when she reached around to undo her bra. I couldn't keep myself from sitting up to meet her and wrapping my lips around her waiting breast.

Darcy held my head to her chest, her hands lost in my hair. She cried out when my teeth pulled her nipple, and I felt another wave of pleasure crash through her body. She pushed my chest back down to the bed, and she wrapped her hand around me again before guiding me to her opening. I kept my eyes on her as she looked down at me and felt her press aside her underwear until I finally felt the warm wetness of her skin against me.

"I wanted this the second I saw you dripping wet in that entryway," I told her. "I wanted to rip off all your clothes and take you right there."

"I wanted you too," she said, a glint in her eye, and then she pressed her hips down fast. I couldn't speak as I felt her surrounding me. She moved down recklessly, pressing me as deep as she could, before lifting back up. My hips lifted to meet hers as she came down again, and we found a rhythm that had our hips crashing together. My hands were on her legs, guiding her up and down as I felt pressure building.

I watched her bounce on top of me, her mouth a round O of pleasure, and brought my hands back to her breasts, eager to bring her release. Darcy groaned as I touched her, and I was delighted to see her hand reach down between her legs. I grew even harder as I watched her touch herself as I moved my length in and out of her. Her breath quickened, and I saw her fingers move faster.

"Keep going," she begged. She fell forward onto her elbow, one hand still working between our bodies as I pressed my hips up with force. I was getting close, but I wanted Darcy to find pleasure as well, so I held back as much as I could while her fingers worked, bringing her closer to completion.

"I'm close," Darcy whispered in my ear, and I almost lost control myself, but I pulled it back. I worked to keep the same rhythm, eager to help her, and suddenly she was shaking over me, her muscles squeezing tight around my erection as she crashed into her pleasure. She cried out, and it was too much for me. I quickly rolled her hips off me as I found my own release and let out a deep growl of ecstasy. I shuddered with each wave of pleasure until I lay still, trying to catch my breath.

We laid still in the darkness of the room. It was only now that I realized we hadn't turned on any lights. It was late now, and the air outside Darcy's windows was dark and quiet. The rain still fell hard and fast, and it was the only sound in the room other than our labored breathing. I reached over to feel Darcy's arm next to mine and I pulled her to me, happy when her head rested on my chest. Her bare chest pressed into my own and I delighted in the warmth I felt as our breathing became in sync.

"I didn't expect that," I said. My voice sounded strange in the quiet of the room.

"Me neither," Darcy said. "But I'm glad you came over." The words pleased me. They were an affirmation that maybe Darcy's feelings for me were changing a bit. Earlier today, when she was begrudgingly showing me warehouses and old garages, I was ready to give up on any hope of a relationship with her. But after tonight, I couldn't help wondering if something had changed.

This morning, I had set out to make Darcy see the real me. After spending the day together, I think she was seeing me for who I was. I thought back to our conversation over dinner. Where we had talked about how hard it was to have so much attention on me. Where Darcy had admitted she could never live like that. It felt like she was understanding a little bit about the man underneath the facade of the rock star.

"I'm glad you invited me," I said. "But just so you know, I didn't expect it. That's not why I bought you dinner." I ran my hand through Darcy's hair and found it was still damp from the rain earlier today.

"*Sure* it wasn't," Darcy said, teasing me. "You're telling me it never crossed your mind?"

"I didn't say that!" I laughed with her. "My mind has been through a lot of fantasies after last night. But I didn't let myself hope. I wasn't expecting anything."

"Fantasies, huh?" Darcy asked, and I heard the interest in her voice.

"Umm-hmm," I said, feeling a stir deep in my stomach. "One of them's no longer a fantasy, though."

"Oh really?" Darcy asked. "Which one?"

"Let's just say it had something to do with that adorable mouth of yours."

I could almost feel Darcy's body flush at the words, and she slipped a leg over my own, pressing herself against my hip.

"You know," Darcy said, running a hand up and down my chest. "It's still raining hard out there."

"It is," I said. I felt both aroused and sleepy, pulled

between a desire to embrace all those beautiful curves of Darcy's body and a need to slip off into rest after a day filled with ups and downs.

"It might not be safe to drive."

They were exactly the words I was hoping to hear, and I smiled as I heard them.

"You're right," I agreed. "It would probably be a bad idea to go home."

With an agreement between us, Darcy shifted to kick the covers of the bed down so we could climb under them. I settled into Darcy's bed and felt her body settle in against me, her leg comfortably around my own and her head back to my shoulder. I gave in to the calming sound of rain falling outside and the warm feel of Darcy beside me.

15

DARCY

I woke to the sun coming through the windows, the rain finally gone. The warm feel of Callum next to me was a welcome presence, and I squeezed him to me ever so slightly. He slept soundly, and I rolled over to slip out of bed, desperate for coffee. I found my sweatpants discarded on the floor and grabbed a sweatshirt that hung on the back of my door before padding downstairs on tiptoes.

I scooped coffee into the coffee pot, remembering to make enough for two of us. After seeing Callum at the coffee shop yesterday, I knew he drank coffee. My mind floated back to last night when we sat at this table talking about Callum's life. It was surprising to hear how much he disliked the spotlight. He did a great job of hiding this fact if the numerous pictures and articles were any indication. But I was realizing that looks can be deceiving.

I checked my phone, which I had left on the kitchen table. As the comforting smell of coffee permeated the room, I took a seat and opened a text from Liz.

Tell me if that brother of mine doesn't treat you right.

I smiled. Liz always seemed to be one step ahead of us. Clearly she understood that Callum's absence from her house last night could only mean one thing.

Nothing to worry about, I shot back.

Instantly, I saw her typing.

Ooooh. Details!

I rolled my eyes. No way was I giving Liz details on what happened last night. We were close, and we had certainly talked about those things before, but I had never dated someone who also knew Liz so closely. It would be too weird to talk to her about her brother in that way.

No way! I shot back.

I had to temper the smile that spread across my face. I felt happy, warm and content from sleeping beside Callum last night. But I knew I couldn't let myself get too comfortable. He was only here for the summer. Even if this relationship (or whatever this was) *wanted* to last beyond the next few months, I knew it would never work. I couldn't live a life on the road, following Callum around with his bandmates. My life was here, and Callum's was out there.

I opened my email, flipping my brain toward work. Checking the business email first thing in the morning was a bad habit I was trying to break, but I hadn't hacked the addiction yet. I scrolled through to see a few inquiry emails, asking about some of our open listings. I would respond to those when I got back to the office. That way I could see our calendar and figure out if Liz or myself could show the homes.

I had another email from the realtor who had submitted an offer on my dad's hardware store. I had denied their offer yesterday, not even countering. But now the realtor was coming back with a new offer $5,000 over the asking price. I groaned as I saw it. These people seemed to have their heart set on buying the property. But they wanted to turn it into some group-fitness gym, filled with spin bikes and kettle-bells. I just couldn't stomach the idea of the place turning into something like that. It felt like it would completely erase what my dad had built.

The truth was, I was still dragging my feet on selling the place. I had put it on the market because it seemed like the right thing to do. I wasn't using the place, and I hated to see it sit completely empty. But I was realizing that the idea of someone else occupying the space was even worse than thinking of the place empty. I wrote back a quick message, explaining that we were no longer taking offers at this time. It was a lie, but I hoped it would send the buyers to look elsewhere.

I sighed as I realized it was time for me to consider taking the place off the market. If I wasn't ready to sell it, then it wasn't right to string potential buyers along.

But the right *buyer might be out there*, I thought.

I had this wild fantasy of someone driving through town and seeing the sign, who would suddenly realize they had always wanted to run a hardware store. They would give me a lowball offer and I would accept, simply glad that the legacy of my family business would go on in the hands of a new family. I knew it was crazy. But some tiny part of me couldn't give up the hope.

The coffee pot beeped, and I went to the cabinet to pull down two mugs. I remembered Callum ordering his coffee black at the cafe. I poured a bit of milk into my own and was about to carry the mugs back upstairs when I heard my phone chime with a new email. I set the mugs down and sat at the table again to open it.

At first, I thought it was another email from the same realtor. The subject line mentioned the hardware store. But when I looked at the name, it wasn't hers. Someone else was emailing about the place, on behalf of a wealthy client. I opened the email and read through the message. Shock coursed through me as I took in the email in front of me. I couldn't shake the feeling of utter betrayal, a sense that I had been right all along about Callum Jones. I stormed upstairs, the coffee forgotten, and shoved open my bedroom door.

"Get out!" I cried. He still wasn't awake, but my voice made him stir. He looked back at me through sleepy eyes, his arms wrapped under his pillow. He gave a bit of a smile as he saw me, clearly not registering the words I had said to him.

"Hey there," he said, but he must have seen the anger in my eyes because his brow creased in confusion.

"Get out!" I said again. I picked up his jeans from the floor and threw them at the bed.

"What's wrong?" he asked, suddenly sitting up. I couldn't take the concern on his face, and I simply gathered the rest of his clothes and shoved them into his arms.

"Darcy," he said, grabbing my arm so he could look at me. But I pulled away from him, yanking my arm out of his grip.

"Don't touch me," I yelled.

"What the hell is going on?" There was a hint of anger in his voice now as he realized he was being unceremoniously thrown out of my house.

"Is this just a joke to you?" I was mad at myself when tears filled my eyes. I didn't want to cry, but I felt hurt and confused as I looked at him. Most of all I was mad at myself for letting myself get carried away last night. For trusting Callum when every part of me knew better.

"A joke?" he asked. He was getting dressed, throwing his

T-shirt over his head. "You're the one kicking me out of your house at eight a.m.—I should be asking you that same question!"

"Did you think I wouldn't see it? Did you think you could send in an offer and someone else would just accept it? Or did you *want* me to see it? Maybe you're doing all this just to hurt me again."

I stormed out, too angry to stay in the same room as him. Rushing down the stairs and into the kitchen, I felt trapped. Pacing back and forth, I wiped tears from my eyes to hide my breakdown. I hoped he would leave through the front door, leaving me in peace. But he was right behind me, rushing into the kitchen.

"Darcy," he said, his voice much calmer. "Will you please tell me what's going on?"

"You know what's going on," I said, my arms crossed as I leaned against the counter.

"I don't. I promise."

"You're trying to buy my hardware store," I spit out. Tears spilled down my cheeks as I said the words. "You know how much that place means to me, and you put in an offer to pull it out from under me!"

"No!" Callum said, walking toward me. He was trying to touch my arm, but I pulled away. The kitchen was too small, and I rushed into the living room, holding my arms tight against my chest.

"Darcy," he said, following me into the room. "I was trying to help you."

"By tearing my dad's legacy apart? I won't let you!"

"Liz told me how special the place is to you. She said no amount of money can replace that love. I totally get that. I just thought that maybe I could get close. Maybe I could offer enough to make you feel alright to sell it."

"And so you offered *double* the asking price?" I asked. It didn't make any sense. My brain swirled with confusion as I tried to work out what was happening. "You weren't doing that for *me*. You were trying to give a number I couldn't say no to. Just so you can have your precious *recording studio*."

"I wasn't!" Callum cried out. "I was just trying to make things easier for you."

"So, you *don't* intend to put a recording studio in there?"

"Of course I do," Callum said. "Why would I buy a building and leave it to sit empty?"

"You see?" I asked, my eyes round as I accused him of something he had just admitted to. "You are out for yourself!"

"I thought it could benefit both of us!" he said back, raising his voice. His body was tense as he observed me, and I sensed his own frustration growing as he looked at me.

"I want you out!" I yelled, and Callum threw up his hands, trying to figure out for the last time what he had done wrong.

"I didn't think this would make you so upset," he said. "I was trying to help."

"I don't know how I let myself trust you," I said. My voice was low and cruel, intended to hurt him. "I knew when we were teenagers you were bad news. I should have known you would never change."

Callum looked back at me, and I thought he might say something. He even took a step forward, ready to continue this argument. But then I saw him close his mouth. He shook his head, and I saw my words had found their mark. He looked hurt, but I kept my face cold and impassive, an unmovable scowl.

Callum turned away and stomped toward the entryway. I followed to watch him grab his coat from the hook, nearly pulling it off the wall in the process. With one final glare at me, he threw open the front door and slammed it behind him. Wanting to see him truly gone, I rushed to the front window and saw him slam into the driver's side of his car. He turned it on and sped away, moving much too fast down the street.

Good, I thought. *Get out of here.*

It had been a mistake to let Callum into my house last night. It had been a mistake to bring down my walls and let him get to know me better. Right then I promised myself it was a mistake I wouldn't make again. Callum Jones had shown me who he really was, and I was finally ready to believe him.

16

CALLUM

"Today we're honored to have musician and recording artist Callum Jones with us! Welcome, Callum."

"Thanks for having me," I muttered, doing my best to force excitement into my voice. I sat stiffly in front of a microphone, headphones pressing too tightly against my ears. After I spoke with my marketing team about how to clear up the confusion regarding my career and my commitment to my band, they arranged a radio interview with a local station. They were hoping other stations and news outlets would pick up the interview, finally clearing up any confusion once and for all.

"We'd like to start with the question that's on everyone's mind: Are you leaving the Horizon?"

"Thanks for letting me clear that up," I said. I had reviewed the talking points my team sent over as I waited in the radio station's lobby. Now I sought to remember the words, wanting to get things right. "I am not leaving my band. I remain committed to the music and artistry of the Horizon and my bandmates."

"So what caused the confusion?" the DJ asked. He was a young guy, called Wesley, with shaggy hair on the top of his head that was shaved along the sides. He wore a nose ring and a lip ring, and I thought I saw the hint of eyeliner around his eyes. He also had a list of pre-approved questions, so we moved through the interview like two actors doing a cold read of our scripts.

"I'm visiting my family this summer, so I'm back in my hometown. I wanted to do something to thank them, so I decided on a concert. My bandmates are on their own vacations right now, and I wasn't about to ask them to join me."

"But what about the new music?"

"As an artist, I'm always working on new material. And a show like this was the perfect opportunity to try some things out ..."

As I continued the speech I'd rehearsed, my mind floated to Darcy. I saw her angry face and the way she was close to tears. I had never meant to hurt her like that, but it was all too clear that I had done completely the wrong thing. I knew now that I shouldn't have put in an offer without speaking to her. But hindsight was twenty-twenty, and I had no idea if she would ever give me the chance to explain myself.

After storming out of her house, I drove much too fast back to Liz's place. After nearly blowing through a stop sign, I forced myself to calm down. I drove carefully with my hands squeezing tight on the steering wheel until I pulled up outside of the house. I was glad to find no one home. It meant I didn't have to explain myself to Liz who would certainly press me for details about where I was last night.

With only forty-five minutes before I had to get to the radio station, I kicked off my clothes and jumped in the shower. The warm water against my skin was rejuvenating, and I felt my muscles relaxing under the warmth. I found parts of my body were sore from my time with Darcy last night, and I couldn't help thinking about Darcy in bed. My mind flashed to her lips surrounding my length, and suddenly I felt a pull deep in my stomach.

I shook my head and pushed the thoughts aside. I didn't have time for that. Allowing myself to give in to fantasies of Darcy would only make me late for my interview. Instead, I switched the water to cold and grabbed the soap so I could finish rinsing off.

"And how are you finding your time back home?" Wesley asked. His words brought me back to the radio station and the interview I was in the middle of completing. I turned on my phone and flipped to the email my team had sent me with the questions. I was relieved to see we were nearly finished.

"It's always wonderful to be home," I said, reading the words from the email. "I try to get back every chance I get." But even as I said them, I realized how false they sounded. It had been years since I was back home, and these words made it sound like a frequent thing. I felt a bit of resentment building in my chest. After all, my manager and my team were the ones who kept my schedule booked with tours and recording sessions and never allowed me to visit family. How hypocritical of them to portray me as some guy popping home every other weekend.

I paused for a moment and Wesley looked at me. He was clearly expecting a longer response, and it was true the team had given me a full paragraph about the people from my hometown being some of the best fans, and how I found inspiration for my writing when I traveled. But I felt rebellion inside of me. I didn't know if it was anger toward my team or deep guilt over how things ended with Darcy this morning, but I was suddenly speaking words that were well off script.

"Actually, Wes, this trip home has been a very meaningful one."

"How so?" Wesley asked. I saw him sit up. He recognized right away that I was abandoning the careful words the marketing team had sent me. He probably saw an opportunity to gain some exclusive information.

"Well, I've met someone."

I could hardly believe I said it. But now that the words were out there, there was no turning back. I could only hope Darcy was listening. Maybe she would hear this and give me a second chance.

"Actually, I didn't just meet her," I clarified. "I've reconnected with someone I knew a long time ago. And she's just as amazing as I remember her."

"Well, now!" Wesley said. "Does this mean the rock star might be settling down? Are you about to break the hearts of millions of girls out there?"

I winced at the words, hating his insinuation that I was a player. But I knew it was the public perception. I heard Brady's voice in my head, telling me that sex sells.

"It means I'm interested in putting down some roots. I've been on the road for a long time without a home base. I've been thinking lately that it might be good to be here a bit more permanently."

"But what would that mean for your band?" Wesley asked.

"It doesn't have to mean anything," I said. Suddenly it felt like I was speaking to my bandmates, trying to convince them that this change didn't need to be a bad thing. "I'll still go out on tour, and we're still planning to write new music and get back into the recording studio. It just means I'll have a home near people I love."

Whoops, I thought. *Was that too far?*

I was thinking of Liz and my niece and nephew when I said it. Would Darcy think I meant something else? Would it scare her even more to believe I was thinking about this? I couldn't dwell on it. Instead, I barreled forward.

"In fact, I'm thinking of opening a recording studio in town."

"Well, that's exciting news!" Wesley said. "You heard it here first, folks, on KNW."

"That way the band could come to Maplewood to record our next album. And it could be a spot for other artists who need time away from the city. We could show others how great Maplewood is. Maybe make this place a true artists' retreat."

"Wow!" Wesley said. "And what's the timeline? When can Maplewood expect more celebrities walking our sidewalks?"

"Well, I found a building I love. I can't get into too many details yet, but it's a property with tons of potential. And a lot of historic elements. That's why I like the place so much, because I can maintain the history of the place and make it unique. This won't be some clean and modern recording studio with no character."

"And you're sure you can't tell us the location? I'm sure everyone in town is dying to know!"

"Not now," I said. I felt a brief panic that I might have said too much. Darcy was already angry at me for putting an offer in on the hardware store. But I thought maybe this interview could show her I didn't want to destroy the thing her father and grandfather built. I saw it as my opportunity to get through to her. I knew she was too angry with me to let me speak to her face-to-face. If she could hear this radio interview, though, maybe I could make her understand.

"Sorry, I can't tell you the details. I want to be respectful of the current owner of the place. The building's been in her family for a number of years, and I would never do anything to disrespect the building or her family. But I can say that I will do everything in my power to make it a building that Maplewood and the family can be proud of."

"Wow! What exciting news from Callum Jones. You heard it here, folks—Maplewood might be the next recording capital of the world! And now, enjoy Callum Jones and the Horizon with their hit single 'Undercover'."

17

DARCY

I clicked off the car radio as Callum's voice sang through my speakers. I was still shocked from what I had just heard, overwhelmed that he would say all of that on the radio. Did this mean he was actually serious about staying in town?

I rolled down my window and breathed in the smell of wet dirt from all the rain yesterday. I let the air rush over my face as I tried not to think about the warm, solid presence of Callum sleeping beside me last night. I was headed to Everett, the town next to ours. An office building had just been listed, and I had a chance to see it before anyone else did.

Liz and I had spent the past six months discussing the possibility of an office space in Everett. It would give us a spot to meet with clients instead of them having to drive out to Maplewood. And, based on market research, the real estate market in Everett was about to explode.

My phone buzzed beside me, and I looked down to see my accountant's name pop up on my cell phone screen. I turned the car sound system back on so I could answer it through Bluetooth.

"Hello?" I asked, rolling up the window so I could hear him better.

"Hey, Darcy, it's Anthony."

"Yeah, hi Anthony," I said. I tried to bring my mind back to any recent conversations I'd had with him about my finances. I hired Anthony after my dad died to help me manage his assets and assist with the closing out of accounts.

"So, you asked me to take a look at things," he said. "So you could think about buying some more property in Everett."

"Right," I said, thankful he was reminding me of what we last talked about. My mind felt scattered, filled with fragments of conversations. "I'm actually on my way to check out a property now."

"You are?" he asked. His voice sounded surprised and even a little nervous. I could tell it was a bad sign.

"What's up?" I asked, trying to keep my voice light.

"I'm not sure it's the right time to invest right now. After closing out your father's estate, there's not as much left as you might have hoped. And you still have the property taxes on the hardware store which aren't insignificant."

"I see," I said. I flexed my fists around the steering wheel. "So, there's not enough there for a down payment?"

"The down payment wouldn't be too much of a problem," he said. I could hear papers rustling on the other end of the phone. "But I'm not sure carrying two mortgages and paying taxes on three properties makes the most sense with your current financial situation. They would be significant expenses to account for each year. Now, if you were to sell the hardware store ..."

"I don't want to talk about that," I snapped. I was instantly embarrassed by this knee-jerk reaction. But any conversations about the hardware store felt far too raw and emotional for me.

"I understand that," Anthony said. "But it's hard to ignore such a big offer."

I held my tongue. I knew if I tried to talk about the hardware store, and the offer Callum had made on it, I might not be able to keep a waver out of my voice. I didn't want to cry in front of my accountant.

"A cash offer like that would completely change your financial situation. You could open *three* offices if you wanted to!"

"We don't want that," I said, keeping my jaw locked in place. Liz and I weren't looking to create some real estate empire. We simply wanted a place where our clients could meet with us close to the properties they were selling or buying. And we wanted to cut down on our own commute time.

"Of course," Anthony said, a hint of apology in his voice. "I just meant it would change things. I wouldn't have any problem advising you to buy in Everett if you accepted the offer on the hardware store."

"I understand," I said. I glanced at the clock, knowing Anthony would charge me for this phone call and dreading the bill. "Is that all?"

"What are you thinking about that offer?" he asked. Even though I had told him I didn't want to talk about it, he was clearly not ready to let this go. "Will you accept it?"

"Like I said, Anthony," I muttered. "I don't want to talk about it."

"Of course," he said. "Anyway, let me know how things

go at the Everett property. If you want to put in an offer, I might have to move some things around."

"Got it," I said. "Thanks for your help."

After I hung up I let out an angry groan, full of frustration and confusion. It was frustrating to hear people speak about the hardware store as simply an asset with a fixed price tag. The memories of that place made it worth so much more to me. But I knew it was hard for other people to understand that. Callum's words floated back to me.

I will do everything in my power to make it a building that Maplewood and the family can be proud of.

Was it true? Would Callum find a way to honor the history of the place? I wanted to believe it, but all my doubts about Callum Jones came flooding back to me. If he wanted to honor my family, then why didn't he tell me he was putting an offer in on the place? Why did he blindside me with that?

I pulled up to the office that was about to be listed and saw the real estate agent standing outside, waiting for me. He was an acquaintance of mine; someone I had interacted with a few times during real estate deals for clients. Liz always joked about how handsome he was, and ever since my break-up, she had been dropping hints to me about going out with him.

"Hey, Darcy." He smiled, and I saw warmth in his eyes. I wasn't sure if I should hug him or not, but we opted for a handshake that lingered a bit too long.

"Hey, Randy," I said.

"It's so good to see you." He smiled down at me before reaching out to open the door and letting me cross in front of him.

"Thanks for letting me look at the place. Liz and I are thinking it might make sense to have an office out here."

"I was curious why you were looking at an office space!" Randy said. "If I had known the competition was coming to Everett, I might have said no to showing you the place." He laughed then, and I was caught by how easy we fell into this playful conversation with one another.

"Don't worry," I said. "From what I hear you've pretty much clinched the market for single, middle-aged women. I don't think Liz and I are going to interfere with that!"

"You underestimate yourself," he smiled.

He showed me the space which was one open room with a conference room off to one side and a kitchen on the other. The open space still held large metal desks lined up in rows that was weirdly reminiscent of a police station. The ceiling had old fluorescent lights that were flickering.

"I know it's not much," Randy said, following beside me as I toured the space. "But with a little work, it could be a comfortable space."

I thought back to Anthony's comments. If it would be difficult for me to scrape together the down payment for the place, it was unlikely I would have the money to renovate. As I listened to Randy explain the parking lot spaces and the rental potential in the space upstairs, I couldn't help feeling discouraged. Liz and I were working so hard for a place like this, and it could really expand our business. But without selling the hardware store it looked like it wasn't an option.

"It might be bigger than what we need," I told him.

"Sure, but you could partner with other real estate agents. You could rent out desk space."

"That's an interesting idea," I said. I wondered what sort of income that could bring in, but I felt weird asking Randy about that. I didn't want to seem too desperate.

"I've had a few other calls about it, but I'll give you first refusal if you want. But I can't let it sit too long or my part-ners will start to ask questions," he joked.

"Thanks, Randy," I said. "I'll talk it over with Liz."

"Absolutely."

There was a pause then, now that the official real estate business was primarily concluded. I took another moment to stare back at the room, and I could feel the very palpable presence of Randy beside me.

"I was sorry to hear about what happened with your engagement," Randy stated.

I blinked at him.

"Which part?" I asked. "The engagement or the breaking up?"

He chuckled at this.

"I meant the breaking up," he said. "Though, maybe 'sorry' isn't the right word. That guy must be an idiot to let you go."

Suddenly the air between us felt tense, filled with unspoken questions.

"Maybe you'd like to have dinner sometime?" Randy asked. "If you're ready to see other people, that is."

My head spun with this question as I stared back at Randy's strong jaw and his short, carefully styled hair. Liz hadn't been wrong to think there might be something between us. And now that I had broken up with John, nothing was stopping me. Right?

I was surprised when Callum's face floated into my brain. The radio interview earlier and his comments about the hardware store were still fresh in my thoughts and then there was dinner and everything else last night. I thought of the casual, easy conversation between us and the spark I felt anytime our eyes connected.

You kicked him out of the house this morning, I reminded

myself. *You were fuming mad at him! And now you're going to let him be the reason you* don't *go on a date with a handsome, successful man you are attracted to?*

I knew I should say yes to Randy. I knew Callum Jones was too complicated and too famous for there to be something real between us. And yet, I couldn't bring myself to go on a date with someone else. Everything inside of me was rejecting the idea.

"I don't think I'm ready for that," I told Randy, echoing his own words.

"No problem," he said. "I totally get it."

As Randy smiled at me, I wondered if I was missing out on some calm, predictable life where I would work alongside my real estate husband. We would join the business association and send our kids to private school.

"Let me show you out," Randy said, pointing me back toward the door.

As he walked me back to my car, I knew it wasn't the life for me. I didn't know what was ahead of me, but I would take a life that was fun and unpredictable over one that was ordinary any day. As I said my goodbyes to Randy, I slipped back into my car and checked my phone. I had a text from Liz staring back at me:

911! Elementary School!

18

CALLUM

"What's going on?" I asked, bursting into the elementary school auditorium. I caught sight of Liz standing up front, placing mouse ears onto a small boy's head. There were boxes in front of her that seemed to be vomiting feather boas and sparkly vests.

"You made it!" Liz said as she spun to greet me. But she immediately caught sight of a long, brown piece of fabric that she pulled out of a bin. "I found the lion's tail!" she cried out. A nearby parent shrieked and came to take it from her.

"Is everything alright?" I asked.

Children were milling about everywhere, and the room was a mess of noise and movement. A woman at the piano was struggling to review a song with a group of children while a parent was putting safari hats onto their heads. Liz and another mother were sorting through the boxes in front of them while two teenagers were on the auditorium's stage erecting two-dimensional trees.

"It's a mess," Liz said. "There was a PTA meeting in here

last night which meant we couldn't install the set until *now*! And the costumes didn't arrive in time! They're stuck in the mail somewhere, so we have to improvise!"

Liz held out her hands to the boxes of costumes in front of her, as if she wanted me to see how difficult it would be for her to salvage something from these plastic tubs. I smirked at her.

"What are you laughing at?" she asked. "This is serious stuff!"

"Oh, absolutely!" I said, feigning solemnity. "A summer camp play about the animal kingdom is not a laughing matter!"

"Make jokes!" Liz said, tossing a fuzzy sweatshirt at me that someone had painted cow spots onto. "But your niece will not be happy if this show is anything less than the Broadway production she's imagining!"

"Alright, alright!" I said, holding up my hands. "I'm here to help."

"Good," Liz said. "No one can figure out how to set up the sound system."

"And you think *I* know how?" I asked, giving her an incredulous look.

"You're a musician!" she said. "You must know something about it!"

"I have people for that," I said to her. "All I have to do is show up for mic check and plug in my guitar."

As another group of children were ushered toward her, Liz glanced at me with exasperation. She smiled at them, eager not to show them any of the stress she was feeling.

"Are these our little bear cubs?" she asked, and the smallest campers nodded at her.

"Please, Callum," she said, glancing over at me as she

pulled brown baseball caps from the bottom of one of the bins. "Can you just try?"

I sighed at her.

"Fine. Let me look at it."

"Thank you!" Liz said. She instantly turned back to the children in front of her as the piano plunked out a rousing number about a hungry tiger. I made my way to the back of the auditorium where an ancient-looking soundboard was sitting on a plastic table. I groaned as I noticed not a single cable was plugged into the board. Whoever tried to set this thing up had given up quickly.

I pulled out my phone and clicked to my YouTube app. When I needed to learn something quickly the site never failed me. But the last video I had searched was still there when I opened the app. It was the video of me playing my solo stuff. And it was up to 1.7 million views. I was about to ignore it and type "Soundboard set up" into the search board, but my eye caught the comments section. I read:

Please make a solo album!

The comment surprised me. I thought most people were upset to think I might be abandoning the Horizon. But this person seemed interested in listening to my own work. I knew that a deeper dive into the comments section could only bring pain, but I couldn't help myself. I read on, jumping over the nasty comments.

So good! Please do an acoustic album. We want more!

On the radio today he said he just played this for fun. Boo! I wish he was actually going to produce a solo album.

We need a petition for a Callum Jones solo album. Who's ready to sign?

I blinked as I scrolled through, seeing more and more likes and positive comments. Were all these people actually interested in me breaking out on my own? Did they actually like my stuff? A slam of the door next to me made me jump, and I looked up to see Darcy striding through the door. I felt a sudden urge to look busy, and I quickly searched for the video of the soundboard set-up. But Darcy didn't see me in the back of the room. I saw her head straight to Liz.

With new nerves as I realized Darcy was here too, I focused on solving the soundboard problem. I wasn't sure if I wanted to talk to Darcy after this morning's screaming match in her living room. And then there were my comments on the radio that I had no idea if she had heard. I kept my head down until I could think things through.

The squeaky sound of children's voices was driving me a little crazy in this echoey space. I didn't have high hopes amplification would make it sound any better, but Liz was counting on me to fix things. I followed along with the video tutorial and unpacked the cords and cables I needed to power up the board and connect it to the speakers that hung at various locations in the room. Next, I set to work on microphones, and I was rewarded with a loud squeak that told me I had succeeded! But the sound caused everyone else in the room to cover their ears.

"Sorry! Sorry!" I cried out as I muted the microphone. Without thinking, I checked in with Liz at the front of the auditorium, and Darcy was staring back at me. My eyes caught hers as she helped a child put on a sparkly vest, but she quickly looked away.

So she didn't hear, I thought. If Darcy was still avoiding me, then it probably meant she didn't hear what I said on the radio. Either that or she wasn't ready to accept my apology. I had a sudden urge to talk to her. I needed her to know I didn't mean to hurt her with the offer. In fact, I thought it would help her. I was trying to show her how much I valued the place since she loved it so much. But how could I find a way to make her understand that?

One of the dads had wandered over to me and the soundboard, looking a little lost. I imagined he had been dragged along by his wife and now he wasn't sure where to help.

"Want to give me a hand?" I asked. As I walked the guy through the soundboard and the set-up of additional hand-held microphones, my eyes floated to the front. I saw Darcy walking onstage to line the kids up. Liz was looking at all of them together and Darcy was adding a hat or a boa wherever Liz instructed.

After a moment, I saw Darcy cross to the backstage area, and I saw my opportunity to catch her alone for a moment.

"I'll be right back," I told the dad, named Ian. "You'll be alright?"

"Sure thing," he said. It was exactly as I expected: He was thrilled to have a task instead of wandering around the room.

Once I knew Ian was comfortable, I took off toward the stage, dodging parents who were setting up folding chairs in neat rows. I pushed my way through the door that led backstage and climbed a few steps to get to stage level. Darcy was there, pinning a tail to the back of a child's costume. When the kid ran back onstage, she turned to look, and she caught me out of the corner of her eye.

"What are you doing?" she asked. She seemed jumpy, as if she didn't know how to react to me.

"Can we talk?" I asked. "Just for a minute."

"Liz needs me," she said, but she didn't make any attempt to move. I took it as a good sign and continued. I might as well get out what I could before she walked away.

"So, the offer," I said, cutting right to the chase. "I wasn't trying to hurt you."

"I don't want to talk about this," Darcy told me. "We have too much to do to get this show ready."

"You don't even have a kid here!" I laughed, and I saw Darcy crack a smile.

"Liz's kids are like my kids," she answered.

"Mine too," I said. She turned to me then, looking at me properly for the first time in the conversation. "Look, if you don't want me to buy the place then I won't. I'll withdraw the offer, no questions asked."

"I'm going to help Liz," she said. Darcy crossed onto the stage then and called out another group from the wings. She lined up the little butterflies and helped them put on their wings as Liz pointed to which kid should get which color.

I watched her for a moment, shaking my head as two of the kids started fighting over the blue pair of wings. While Darcy tried to be gentle with them, Liz interrupted the argument with a quick threat, telling them they wouldn't get any wings if they didn't calm down. I laughed, but Liz's reprimand was effective, and they were able to continue. I left as the kids were given matching headbands with bouncing antennae on them.

The conversation with Darcy had been brief and inconclusive. She hadn't said anything when I told her I would withdraw my offer on the hardware store. Was that a sign that she didn't want me to? Or was she still too mad to talk to me about it? I shuffled back to the soundboard as I tried to interpret every brief interaction Darcy and I had.

At least she didn't yell, I thought. That was certainly an improvement from this morning. And when I thought about it, I felt a softness from her that was a far cry from open hostility. So maybe she was willing to forgive me after all.

"You okay, man?" Ian asked as I joined him back behind the table.

"What would you do if you liked someone, so you put in an offer on her family property that's way over the asking price, but then she gets upset you did it?"

"What?" Ian asked. He looked at me blankly, clearly overwhelmed by all the information I had just laid at his feet. The man had only just learned how to do sound. I guess it was too much to expect him to be a confidant when I had only just met him.

"Never mind," I answered. I clicked the headphone jack into the laptop being used for sound and heard children's music blast out through the speakers. The children cheered as they heard the familiar tracks they had worked with for the past week. I waved at them and gave them a mock bow amidst their clapping. When I rose from this bow, I looked across the room and saw Darcy staring back at me.

19

DARCY

"Why did you do this?" I asked, returning to Liz's side. "Why invite me here when you know Callum's here too?"

I had called Liz immediately after Callum drove away from my house. I knew she would see the offer on the store soon, since it was in both of our inboxes, and I needed her to hear the information from me. But it meant she also forced some of the other details out of me. She had prodded until I told her that Callum spent the night last night. I was upset when she was giddy about it, seemingly ignoring my outrage.

"Didn't you hear his radio interview this morning?" Liz asked as someone practiced closing the theater's red curtain. While it closed, all the kids waved at Liz and me who stood on the auditorium floor off of the stage.

"I heard it," I mumbled.

"Okay! So you know it was just a misunderstanding. He wants to preserve your family legacy. He was only trying to help!"

"By tearing apart the store and making it some big musician's paradise? That probably means drinking and doing drugs long into the night. He might think Maplewood wants that, but he's sorely mistaken."

Liz's eyebrows bent down in a frown.

"Is that really what you think all musicians are like?" she asked. "I think you have a simplified version. They are people, you know."

"I know that," I said defensively. Liz was probably right. I had to admit, I was carrying around some stereotype of what musicians were like, though to my credit, it was perpetuated by the media. Seeing people doing drugs to gain their artistic edge, I imagined a recording studio lobby filled with girls waiting for attention from famous people. I envisioned my dad's hardware store as some morally bankrupt building where people went for debauchery. It was the worst-case scenario, but I couldn't shake it from my mind. "Look, maybe you should talk to him," Liz said.

I glanced back to the sound table where Callum was standing with another man and showing him some of the knobs and buttons on the console.

"Unless you're not interested in him. And if that's the case, Darcy, then it's time to put the man out of his misery."

I thought back to earlier when Randy had asked me on a date. Something inside of me had made me say no. Something was telling me that whatever Randy had to offer wasn't right for me. Was that because I wanted a life with someone else?

The thought hit me hard, and I quickly looked away from Callum. Liz was pushing the costumes back into the plastic tubs and pushing them off to the side. The kids were going to do a run through of the show before eating pizza and then setting up for the performance tonight. As she grabbed another box, she looked at me, waiting for a response.

"I don't know what I want," I said; but then, because I needed to try out the words, I said, "I *am* interested in him."

"I know you are!" Liz said, smiling at me, and I rolled my eyes at her. She always thought she could read my mind. And to be honest, many times she was right. "So, get over yourself and see what this could be. If you don't want him to renovate the hardware store, then tell him that. And if you want a hand in what those renovations look like, then I *know* he would let you. *You* have the power here, Darcy."

I listened to Liz's words carefully. It was like I could finally see the situation clearly. All along I had had the power to reject his offer on the hardware store. So why did I get so angry about it? Was it because he threatened to destroy my dad's legacy, perhaps? But some part of me wondered if I was upset about more than that. Was I pushing back against Callum's attempts to get closer to me?

From the beginning I had assumed Callum was only looking for a fling. I thought he would sleep with me and move on, preparing for his next tour and forgetting all about Maplewood. But when I thought back to all our interactions, I wondered if that was a reality I had pushed onto him. In the same way I was holding on to the worst stereotypes of musicians, had I pushed a story onto Callum that was false?

"Will you be alright?" I asked, looking back at the stage where the kids were lining up for their first number.

"I think we put out most of the fires," Liz laughed. "It may not be perfect, but they'll have a show tonight. Thanks so much for your help."

"Of course," I said. I kept my eye on Callum, hoping he wasn't about to rush out of the room now that I had resolved to talk to him.

"Go talk to him," Liz smiled, giving me a gentle shove on the shoulder. "But make sure you're back here for the performance. Maggie and Alan will never forgive you if you miss it!"

"I'll be here," I assured her. I gave Liz a hug and told her how amazing she was for helping her kids, and all the others, put on this show. Then I was gone, crossing to the back of the room as butterflies fluttered around in my stomach. I had no idea what I would say to Callum, but I forced one foot in front of the other until he noticed me coming and gave me a smile.

"Think you got it?" he asked the man standing next to him.

"I'll give it a go," the man said. Callum switched places with him, encouraging the man to take the primary position behind the board.

"Use the run-through as a practice round," Callum explained. "And let me know if you have any problems. I'll check back in to help before the show starts."

"Sure thing," the man said. He nodded at Callum and then glanced at me to give me a slight smile. Callum grabbed his coat from the back of the chair and led me a few feet away where we could have a bit of privacy.

"Could we talk?" I asked. Loud notes from the piano pounded out across the auditorium and the children thundered onto the stage with loud footsteps.

"Let's go outside," Callum laughed. He pushed open the door at the back of the room and we found ourselves in an elementary school hallway. Colorful bulletin boards and children's art covered the walls.

"Were you serious about the things you said on the radio?" I blurted out, unable to hold this in anymore. Callum's eyebrows rose in surprise.

"You heard it?" he asked. I nodded.

"I heard it," I said. "Was it true? Are you ... looking to settle down, or whatever you said?" My words were dismissive, as if I needed to give him an opportunity to back out of this.

"I meant it," he insisted, holding my gaze. "Whatever this is between us, it's different than anything I've ever felt before. And I want to see what's here."

"You're only here for the summer. What about when you have to go back out on the road?"

"You're right," he admitted. At least he wasn't denying it. "We have flights already booked and ticket holders that would be quite upset if we suddenly canceled all their tickets. But we have time off. I want Maplewood to be my home base. I want to come here anytime they send us home."

"And the store?" I asked. My words were still tight and guarded. I couldn't bring myself to believe what he was telling me. Some part of me still believed he was simply trying to trick me into giving up the hardware store. It didn't matter that there wasn't much logic to this. I couldn't stop worrying that his actions were somehow selfish and designed to hurt me.

"I meant what I said. I should have talked to you about it first. The truth is, I talked to my lawyer about it, and before I knew it, there was an offer. I really thought I could make you feel better about selling."

"It's not about the money," I said. "It's never been about that."

"No, I know that." Callum dropped his head. "It was dumb of me to think that offering you more money would somehow make up for all the memories you have of that place. But I wanted to make it easier for you. If you don't want to sell, I totally get it."

"And the plans for the recording studio?"

"I really do want to do that!" Callum said. "If there's a spot to record here, then it means more time at home. More time with the people I care about."

His words from the radio interview echoed through my head: *I'll have a home near people I love.*

"I've been in a lot of recording studios that are cold and dark. It's supposed to be a place to inspire creativity. A place to take risks and allow musicians to find the true sound and feel of their song. I want to help people find that."

His eyes sparkled as he spoke of the place. It was an excitement and energy I hadn't seen from him before.

"You've really thought about this," I said.

"It was only a distant thought when I first came here. But then I met someone."

My breath caught in my throat as he said it.

"And the more time I spent with you, the more I saw a future here in Maplewood."

Callum took my hands in his own, and I felt the warmth radiating through him as he tried to express his feelings to me.

"I love my music," he continued. "And I can't imagine a world without being able to express myself through songs. I never imagined I would care about anything else except my music. But everything changed this summer. I'm starting to think there's room for other things in my life. Music isn't enough anymore. Call me selfish, but I'm ready to love more than just that."

I felt my heart leap in my chest as he said this. He leaned down and kissed me then and I felt how cautious he was. He was asking me a question with that kiss, and I wasn't quite ready to give him the answer. I kissed him back, but I was tentative, and Callum could feel it. He pulled away and waited for me to speak.

His words were racing through my head, and I felt overwhelmed by the information. Something inside of me was holding back, still skeptical. I knew Liz would say my breakup with John had left me less trusting of others. I could almost hear her words echoing through my head. But Liz and I were different people. She was quick to trust. For me, I needed proof.

"Let's go," I said, pulling on his sleeve. I walked down the hall and hoped he would follow me.

"Where are we going?" he asked. "Doesn't Liz need us?"

"We'll be back in time for the show," I assured him. He followed me outside to the school parking lot. "Do you have your guitar?" I asked, turning back to him.

"My guitar? It's in my trunk."

"Grab it," I said. I fished out my keys and unlocked my car as he rushed to his own. He moved his guitar from his trunk to my back seat before jumping into the car with me. He didn't ask me again where we're going, but I felt his eyes on me as I drove and couldn't miss the slight smile on his face as he embraced this next adventure.

20

CALLUM

"Okay, so show me."

I stared back at Darcy. We had just walked through the door of the hardware store and now we stood, looking out into the room. My guitar sat on the floor next to me.

"Show you what?" I asked.

"What you want to do with the place," she said. "Describe it to me."

I blinked at her. Did this mean she was willing to sell the place to me? I felt a surge of nerves to be put on the spot like that. What sort of detail was she looking for? But then I remembered how much I had dreamed about this place. I remembered that I *did* know what I wanted to do. It was time to sell Darcy on the idea.

"Alright," I said, starting slowly. "Well, this door will stay right where it is," I said, gesturing to the front door.

"Very funny," she said, her voice dry and sarcastic. I smiled at her.

"I mean the actual door itself," I explained. "I won't

switch it out or anything." We both glanced back at the door with its embossed writing: *Stevens Hardware.*

"You'll keep the 'Stevens Hardware'?" she asked.

"Yes," I said. "I want people to know what the place was. And if we keep it, then the first thing they see will tell them this place is different."

I saw her smile and knew my first detail had passed the test. Now to the more difficult parts ...

"This area will be the lobby," I said, opening my arms to the front part of the store. "These windows are too nice to cover over, so we'll leave them. Imagine some couches and seating areas. A spot where people can work on some lyrics or just wait for their sessions."

I crossed to a corner, where some low shelves were built into the wall.

"We can leave these built-ins," I told her. "I'd turn this into a coffee bar, and we can keep books on the shelves. And then there's the counter." I crossed back to the center of the room where we both looked back toward the checkout counter.

"What about the counter?" she asked, her voice full of skepticism. I knew that space meant a lot to her. She probably had memories of her dad checking people out behind it. Or even her grandfather.

"We'll keep it," I said, starting with the easy part. "But I'll have to move it."

"It's built into the wall!" she protested. The counter was probably as old as the building itself. It was true that it was practically an extension of the wall next to it, curving around to make an L-shape that someone could stand behind.

"I know," I said. "But they'll be careful with it. I need to move it up front to this lobby area because the back half of the room has to be used for the recording booths."

She didn't respond to this, but simply regarded me carefully. I saw her eyes move from the counter to the front of the room, imagining it moving there. We walked through the center of the room, passing through aisles of hardware goods.

"Imagine this as a hallway," I proposed. "With walls on either side. There would be a door that leads into the control room for the technicians to mix and record. And then the main studio for the musicians and their gear. We'll have drums set up over here and hook-ups for all their instruments. And only the best microphones and mixing equipment."

I felt my words coming faster, overcome with excitement about what the place would look like. I could see it so clearly in my mind's eye. When I looked back at Darcy, she was smiling at me.

"You've really thought about this, haven't you?"

"I think we can fit two of them—one on either side of the hallway. And then two smaller rooms for voice-over work or small recording projects."

I saw her looking around, trying to imagine what I was envisioning.

"I want to keep some of these old signs on the walls. I don't want to erase what this place was. That's the fun of it! A converted hardware store. Like I said, I want this place to be unique and unlike any other studio. It's what will draw people here."

I waited, wondering what she would say about it. At least she hadn't stormed out of the building yet. It seemed like a positive sign, so I gave her a moment to process it all. I didn't want to push too much or move too quickly.

"And you think people will like that?" she asked. "They won't mind that you're keeping some of the historic touches? What if you decide to change it all after a year or something?"

"They'll love it!" I assured her. "Some of the most famous recording studios were converted from garages or non-traditional spaces. The history is what gives it character! It's what lets creativity thrive."

"And what sort of people will you bring here?" Darcy asked. "What sort of music?"

"Any music that speaks to an audience and makes them feel less alone," I said. It had always been why I made music. "I want to produce music that people connect to. Whatever genre that is."

"So you're a producer now?" Darcy asked. I hadn't realized the word had slipped out of my mouth—but when I heard it echoed back to me, I realized it might be exactly what I was interested in.

"That sort of thing would be a long way off," I told her. "After we get the recording studio up and running maybe we could transition into a label of our own. It would let me find new talent that wouldn't otherwise be discovered. I might even find musicians right here in Maplewood!"

"What else?" she asked. She seemed to understand the vision, and I watched her relax into the idea. I saw her looking around, imagining the people who would walk through the door and breathe new life into the space.

"We could do open mic nights," I said. "It's why I want the lobby to be so big. And we'll offer classes for kids who want to learn about recording studios and mixing music or audio engineering. Of course, I'll have to hire some professionals." I laughed as I thought about watching YouTube videos to set up Liz's sound system. If I had professionals working here, then Liz would never have to worry about speakers and microphones again.

"And what about you?" Darcy asked. "Will you still make music?"

With all my plans to make this a thriving cultural center and artists' hub it was easy to forget about my own work. I felt warmth flow through me as Darcy questioned this, as if she wanted to remind me why I started thinking about this recording studio in the first place.

"I want a solo career," I told her. I had spent so long denying this, trying to assure the world that I wasn't leaving the Horizon, that it felt strange to say these words out loud. But then I felt relief wash over me. I knew all at once that I couldn't deny this truth anymore.

"I want to record an acoustic album of my new songs. It'll be a test drive for the new studio. My first album."

"Show me," she said. I looked around the room, thinking she wanted even more details about what the space was going to look like.

"What do you mean?" I asked. "There's nothing else to show. Just the lobby space, the hallway, and the studio spaces."

"No," she said, smiling at me. She crossed back to the front door, and I saw my guitar case sitting on the ground. She picked it up and held it out to me. "Show me."

So, this was what she had in mind. I suddenly understood why she had asked me to bring my guitar along. The request felt intimate, and I had an initial instinct to say no. I had performed in front of hundreds and thousands of people, but an audience of one was much more intimidating. Especially in front of Darcy. But I pushed down those feelings and took the case from her.

I placed it on the ground and took out my guitar.

"Well, the studio will be about here," I said. I crossed to an aisle that held dog food and other pet supplies. Darcy smirked, and I wondered if she would laugh about my surroundings, but she composed herself and stood a bit away, leaning against the shelf as she watched me.

I couldn't think of what to play. I didn't know what she was expecting from me. Should I choose one of the Horizon's hit songs? They would sound very different on an acoustic guitar. I had a feeling it wasn't what was expecting after all this talk about my solo career.

And then, all at once I knew what I would play.

"This one's not even finished yet. But it's something I've been working on."

"Great," Darcy said. She was watching me with a straight face as if she were a music producer putting me through my paces at an audition. "And does it have a title?"

"A working title," I said. "It's called 'Coming Home'."

I saw the slight surprise on her face as I strummed the first chord on my guitar. These lyrics had been floating around in my head for days, though I hadn't put them down on paper yet. But somehow I knew the song was almost finished, even though I had only composed it in brief moments of quiet when my mind was allowed to wander.

I closed my eyes, feeling too exposed with Darcy looking at me, and let myself disappear into the music. The chords that had only existed in my head sounded even better than I imagined, and suddenly I opened my mouth and allowed the lyrics to flow. I sang about long-lost memories in my hometown and seeing things differently through adult eyes. I sang about learning what mattered to me and the cost of fame. And then I sang about the "girl next door" who opened my eyes to what home really meant.

"It's not finished," I said, as I opened my eyes and looked

back to her. I had worked out the chorus and the first few verses, but I hadn't found the resolution yet. "I don't know how the story ends."

Her face was soft, and full of surprise. I could tell I had touched her, and I was glad she understood that this song was all about her and what she had done to me.

"It's beautiful," she said. Her eyes seemed to sparkle, as if she were fighting back tears.

"It's about you, you know," I confirmed. I wouldn't let her think otherwise. I wanted her to know how much she meant to me, and I wouldn't let her question that.

"I kind of got that," she laughed. She moved closer to me and then her hand was on my face, forcing me to look into her eyes. She kissed me, my guitar pressed between us, and there was something celebratory and exciting in that kiss. I could see us here months from now, after the renovations were complete. I could see us locking up the studio late at night and making out in the hallways after everyone went home.

"What do you think?" I asked, pulling back from her. "Did I convince you?"

Her expression changed then, and I realized I had pushed too hard. I couldn't rush her. I needed her to come to this decision all on her own. Darcy crossed away from me and went back to the front of the hardware store. She stared out of the floor-to-ceiling windows and took in the people walking down Main Street. The day was passing from afternoon to evening, and we stood and watched as people left work and locked up their shops to go home for dinner.

I stood next to her in silence, willing to be patient. It dawned on me that I was prepared to wait for Darcy for as long as long as it took. In fact, I was starting to think that I had always been waiting for her.

21

DARCY

"I can't sell it to you," I said, spinning around to face him. I saw his face fall as he took in the words, and I felt a stab of guilt as I saw I had disappointed him.

"I get it," he said. Callum walked his guitar back to the case and began packing it away. He was avoiding my gaze as he did it. "This place is important to you. I understand you don't want someone coming in and replacing it with a whole other business."

"I didn't say that," I said, stepping closer to him. Callum looked up from where he was bent over his guitar case, snapping the latches into place. I forced myself to hold back the smile I felt bubbling inside of me, but I think he saw my smirk because he stood up, his face suspicious.

"What is it?" he asked.

"I just said I can't sell it to you. But that doesn't mean we can't come to some sort of agreement."

Hope flashed into his eyes, and I saw a smile spread across his face.

"An agreement, huh?" he asked. "What sort of agreement?"

"How about a lease?" I asked. "You can rent the building from me. And I'll give you permission to make the renovations."

"I see," he said. Callum stepped closer so we were inches away, the heat building once more between us. "So, I get to pay you rent *and* pay for the renovations? What sort of deal is that?"

"The deal I'm offering," I teased, trying to keep my voice stern as we played at this negotiation. Callum's hands reached out to my hips, and he pulled me against him so my legs pressed against his.

"You're a tough negotiator," he said, his voice barely above a whisper. He bent down and kissed me, pulling my hips further into him. I was desperate to melt into this embrace and see where it would lead us, but a small voice in the back of my mind told me to exercise restraint. We hadn't finished with the business arrangements, and I needed to be sure Callum understood what I was agreeing to before we celebrated.

I pulled away from the kiss and tried to step back, but his hands held me tight. He looped his fingers through the belt loops of my jeans and put on a goofy grin that told me he wasn't about to let me go.

"We have more to talk about," I said, attempting to keep my voice firm. I was trying to be responsible and act like an adult instead of some excited teenager who was only thinking about making out.

"So, talk," he said with a little shrug. I looked into those dark eyes and the hair that was always falling into his eyes. I brought my hands up to his chest and playfully pushed him away.

"Not like this," I laughed. "I can't think!"

"Then how?" he said. "You tell me how you want to negotiate!"

There was an ease and an openness to him that made me feel giddy as I spoke to him. Callum seemed lighter somehow, and I couldn't help catching that sense of excitement and possibility that seemed to radiate out from him. He seemed genuinely excited about turning this place into something, and I felt hopeful that I would get to come along for the ride.

"Come to the office," I said. My dad's office hadn't been used in ages. I pictured the paperwork piled up on the desk and the bankers' boxes that cluttered the floor. But it was somewhere we could sit and put a bit of distance between us.

"Lead the way," he said.

I turned and crossed to the back, trying not to worry about how I put each foot in front of the other. Knowing Callum was right behind me, watching me, made me feel like I no longer understood how to move my body. I pushed away the impulse to look back over my shoulder and simply continued past the checkout desk and shoved my way through the door that was marked "Staff Only".

I couldn't help thinking about the first day Callum was in the hardware store. I remembered the lights clicking off and fumbling my way back to the utility closet. I remembered the excitement I felt to know he was standing so close behind me, shining a light on the fuse box. And I remembered that first kiss ...

I shook off the memory and crossed into the office, feeling Callum directly behind me. The office was even messier than I remembered, with tons of floor space taken up with my dad's paperwork. I knew cleaning out this office was a project I would need to tackle soon but, in that moment, I simply pretended not to see the boxes precariously stacked around the room. Luckily the desk was relatively clean, and I took a seat in my dad's faded-leather rolling chair. I could smell Callum's aftershave as I sat down, the scent wafting out around me.

"We should make it official," Callum joked from the doorway, though I wasn't sure what he meant. Suddenly he knocked on the doorframe, as if I didn't know he was standing there.

"Excuse me, I'm here to discuss a leasing opportunity with you."

Callum bent his head down to play the submissive and eager tenant. I rolled my eyes at him.

"Just sit down," I laughed. "You're being ridiculous."

He rushed in and took a seat across from me. I saw him glance around at the room with amusement.

"I know, I know," I said, catching his gaze. "I need to clean it out. I just haven't gotten to it yet."

"Now I know why you don't want to sell," he said. "You can't face all the cleaning!"

"It's definitely part of it!" I said, and, though it was a joke, there was truth to it. If I sold or even rented the store, I would have to get rid of all the items inside of it. Suddenly I was thinking about weeks of cleaning and sorting and throwing things away. Logistics such as dumpsters and rental trucks started flowing through my head.

"I can help with that," Callum offered, as if he could read the worry on my face. "You don't have to clean it out by yourself."

"Thanks," I said, giving him a small smile. I felt a sudden sadness at the prospect of it all. "It's something I should have done a long time ago."

Callum nodded at me, and I was grateful for the sympathy I saw on his face. But all this talk of cleaning made me realize we needed to discuss timeline.

"Speaking of the cleaning," I said, "it's going to take me some time to clear this place out. I don't know when it will be ready to hand over the keys."

"That's alright. We can go at your pace. I don't want to rush you into anything."

The words felt too apt for our own relationship, or whatever this was brewing between us, and I looked away from his intense gaze.

"Maybe by the end of the summer we'll be ready to start on the renovation," he suggested.

"I'd like some say over things," I said, looking down at my hands that I held clenched in my lap. "I know this recording studio is your dream, but I'd like to see more detail on what you plan to do with the place. And maybe give some input."

"Of course. I don't want to do anything you don't approve of. I really do want to keep the magic of this place. We should make a place we're both proud of."

I looked up at the words, surprised by how open he was being.

"You look surprised," he said. "Were you expecting me to fight you?"

"I don't know," I admitted. "I thought you might want more ... creative control or something. Or free rein of the place."

"I don't need free rein," Callum said. He was gazing back at me, and his voice sounded serious, as if he needed me to understand something. "You're giving me a great gift here, Darcy. I'm not going to take advantage of that. You can be as involved as you want to be. If you want the final say over every decision in the place, then just say the word!"

"Please, no!" I laughed. "I have enough things to worry about with my own business. But I'll appreciate being kept in the loop. And having a glimpse of the plans before you start constructing walls or knocking things down."

"Of course. And the rent—no friends and family discount or anything like that. You have a mortgage to cover and taxes to pay. You should charge me accordingly."

"No mortgage," I said, shaking my head. "I think my grandfather paid that off. We own the building outright." I stopped myself as I heard the word: *We*. With my dad gone, there was no "we" anymore. It was just me. The building and everything inside were my responsibility. Well, mine and Callum's if he agreed to renovate the place.

"Even so," Callum said, "a place like this, right on Main Street, should have a competitive monthly rent. And God knows I can afford it."

"I don't think that's a good thing to be admitting to your new landlord," I laughed.

"My landlord?" he asked, mischief in his eyes. "I like that."

There was innuendo in his voice, though I didn't give myself time to think about what he was getting at. I was still wrapping my head around how this might work and what I needed to make him understand before we shook hands on this deal or wrote up an agreement.

"Don't get too excited," I scolded. "I want to make sure we're not making a mistake here. We might be crazy to get into this."

Callum shrugged, brushing aside my comment.

"I've done a lot of crazy things in my life."

"No, I'm serious," I said. I felt a churning unease in my stomach as my mind imagined everything that might go wrong. What if we started this project and couldn't agree on what should be done to the space? And did committing to this project mean committing to Callum? And then there was that date all those years ago. Callum had abandoned me once—how did I know he wouldn't do it again?

Before my mind could spin out into terror, I took a breath and tried to ask him.

"Getting into something like this ... it's a commitment. And it's something we should both be ready for."

I was pleased that my voice didn't shake as I got these words out. I kept my eyes on Callum's face, trying to read his expression, but he looked stoic. His characteristic smirk was no longer on his face.

"I'm serious about this, Darcy," Callum said. "I meant it when I said I was ready to settle down. That there are people here I care about and that I want to be with."

His gaze was intense, and it seemed like he was telling me he wanted to commit. Did he want to give whatever was between us a chance? But I couldn't stop wondering if I could trust him. I couldn't stop thinking about the past and the times he had let me down.

"And what if that changes?" I asked. My voice was small as I said it, filled with uncertainty and the fear of pain. I forced myself to look at him and, when my eyes caught his, Callum stood up from his seat. He put his hands on the edge of the desk to lean closer to me.

"I'm not running away, Darcy," he whispered. "I've been running away from my past for far too long. It's time for me to see what's right in front of me. It's time for me to see what's been staring me in the face for all this time."

He was inches away from me, and I felt a flutter of warmth flush through me at his words. I couldn't speak. Instead, I leaned forward and pressed my mouth into his, finally allowing myself to say yes to the man standing in front of me.

22

CALLUM

Her kiss took me by surprise, but I wasn't about to reject it. I had been eager to kiss her since we came into this store. And ever since I played her that song, ever since she agreed to let me rent the building, I could hardly think of anything except taking her in my arms. It felt like a commitment of sorts, this arrangement between us, and I hoped that it meant more than just a long-term home for my business. I hoped it meant Darcy and I had a future ahead of us.

I opened my mouth and felt her tongue press into me. She seemed eager, pressing hard against my mouth with an urgency that sent waves of pleasure through me. I pressed back, but it was strange to kiss her over the desk where my legs were pressing hard into the wood as I tried to get closer to her.

"Come here," I said when I pulled my mouth away. I grabbed her arm and guided her around the desk so she stood in front of me. Her face turned up, practically begging to be kissed, but before I took her mouth against my own, I brought my hands to her hips. I lifted her up, so she sat on the edge of the desk and was delighted when she let out a little scream of protest.

"What are you doing?" she asked, but I didn't respond. Instead, I bent down and kissed her even as my hands pressed open her legs so I could stand snuggly between them. She laughed through our kissing, and I felt her smile against my lips. And then her hands were on my back, pulling me closer to her.

Darcy wrapped her legs around me so she could pull me tighter against her. I felt desire flush down between my legs as she pressed herself against me, gently rocking on the edge of the desk.

"My God," I whispered. I pressed back and was sure she could feel how she was turning me on. My mind was awash with images of Darcy spread out over this desk, looking up at me with an eager need as I pressed my length into her. I groaned at the fantasy and took her lip between my teeth, gently biting before releasing her.

"What are you thinking about?" she asked.

"Laying you across this desk," I told her. A flash of surprise crossed her face, but it quickly settled into desire.

"I'd like that," she whispered back, as if she were shy about saying the words. It was too much for me, and I reached down to grab the hem of her shirt and quickly pull it up and over her head. She laughed again, but she grabbed the back of my T-shirt and pulled to expose my chest. She threw it across the room, and I saw the shirt land on a pile of boxes in the corner.

I had stepped back to look at her, but it was Darcy who was taking me in. She had her bottom lip between her teeth, and she was dragging her eyes down my chest. I saw those eyes settle at the bulge between my legs, and I swear I got harder as she looked at me.

"God, I want you," I groaned. I brought my hands to the narrowest part of her waist and ran them up and over her breasts, gently squeezing. Then I pushed her bra down so I could tease her nipples which were already hard and alert, responsive to my touch.

"I wanted you as soon as you sang that song," Darcy said. She gasped when I brought my mouth to her neck, nibbling and licking from her ear to her collarbone. "I couldn't think about anything except taking you right then and there."

Darcy's hand was along the waistband of my jeans, and I shivered as she ran her fingers along my hip bones, dropping below the fabric of my briefs. I bent down to bring my mouth to the nub of her nipple and heard the satisfied sigh as my tongue ran across it. Darcy popped the button of my jeans and lowered my zipper as I switched my mouth to her other breast. She pushed my jeans down to below my hips so she could press her warm hand against my length, still trapped by my underwear.

"See what you do to me?" I asked as she traced the outline of my erection with her fingers. I shivered and stepped away for a moment to kick off my shoes and step out of my jeans before walking back to her. I moved a stack of papers that sat on the desk and then grabbed Darcy's legs so I could spin her to sit on the short edge of the desk.

"Lay down," I ordered, and Darcy obeyed, quickly leaning back so she rested on her elbows where she could watch me. I started with her shoes, removing them one by one, and then went back to her jeans. I undid them and pulled hard at the legs to take them off of her, revealing a pair of black underwear that made me wonder if she was waiting for this. Had Darcy been thinking of this possibility? I certainly had.

This thought made me desperate for her, eager to feel

just how much she wanted this. I pulled at her underwear, and she responded by lifting her hips off the desk, fully exposing herself to me. She lay out on the desk, her gaze fixed on the space between us. I started with a hand on her knee, but then I stepped in to bring my other hand to her inner thigh. I crept closer until I was teasing the wetness that I could see between her legs. Darcy moaned and shifted forward, begging me for more, and I pressed my finger between her lips. As I thought, she was wet and eager for me, and I had to force myself to keep my focus on Darcy and her pleasure even when I wanted nothing more than to take her then and there.

Instead, I rubbed my finger up and down to tease her, watching the way her eyes squeezed closed in pleasure, and then I quickly switched my hand for my mouth. I steadied my hands on the edge of the desk as I bent down to lick her. My tongue pressed against her and Darcy cried out as I slowly experimented with my pace and pressure. As I moved my tongue faster against her, I could tell it wouldn't take long. She was close to the edge before I even touched her, and now my tongue was running circles over the spot I knew would bring her pleasure. I glanced up to see Darcy reach behind her back to unlatch her bra, and then she was touching her nipples, bringing even more pleasure, as I felt her body stiffen beneath my attention.

"Keep going," she said, her voice breathy, and I obliged, doubling down on my efforts. I brought my finger up to tease her opening, and then I pressed deep even as my tongue continued to work between her legs. Almost immediately her whole body was shaking, and Darcy was crying out with abandon. I felt her crash over the edge of pleasure and her legs squeezed hard, trapping my face between them. I kept my finger moving in and out of her as she rode the wave of pleasure until she pushed my head away when it became too much for her. I rested my forehead on her abdomen as she breathed hard, trying to catch her breath, and I was rewarded with small ripples of pleasure that continued to pass through her.

"My God, I needed that," she sighed. The words brought my thoughts to my own need, still stiff and waiting. Darcy seemed to think of this as well, because she tapped my cheek, and I looked up at her. She smiled down at me, and then she shifted her body, jumping down from the desk. I was disappointed for a moment, thinking this fantasy of taking her across the desk wouldn't play out for me, but then she turned around and laid the top half of her body across it. My length jumped as I saw her look back over her shoulder, an invitation in her eyes.

I pressed my briefs down and kicked them off before taking myself in my hand. I stepped up to the perfect woman in front of me and lined myself up between her lips once more. She was still wet and eager, and Darcy spread her legs to give me more access as I found her opening. She arched her back, and I couldn't wait a second longer to slide into her. I pressed in, feeling every inch of her expand to me as I found myself deeper than I had been before.

"God, yes!" Darcy cried out. Her arms reached out to grasp the edges of the desk, and I pulled out before entering her again, delighting in the feel of this angle. But I couldn't go slowly. I was too ready, and the image of Darcy flat on the desk was threatening to undo me. I began rocking back and forth and saw Darcy's body slide up and down along the desk as I did. She gripped her hands harder and tried to hold herself in place, and then I was moving faster, groaning in pleasure as she called out beneath me.

"You feel amazing," I told her, but then I couldn't speak. I took hold of Darcy's hips, and I pulled her against me, driving my length even deeper inside of her. I lost myself in the rhythm of it, and all too quickly I found myself at my edge. One more push and I crashed over the threshold with a cry. Darcy was calling out beneath me as well, and then she was shaking as we both found release. I felt her squeeze against me, drawing even more pleasure, and I collapsed against her back, my forehead wet with sweat.

We stayed like that for a moment, delighting in the sensations running through us. I felt elated, filled with love and admiration for this woman, and I could only hope it would last. I could only hope this was the beginning of something that would continue long after the summer was over.

#

Somehow, we found our way to the floor, pushing aside papers and boxes to make room for our bodies. I thought we were finished with our lovemaking but, after a few minutes of holding Darcy tight against my chest, I kissed her. It started sweet and gentle, but soon it deepened, and I felt the familiar tinge of desire flooding through me. I think we were both surprised when I grew ready again, and we made love gently this time, with Darcy rocking her hips above me and staring down into my eyes. I wanted to tell her I loved her. I wanted her to know what I felt about her, but I was too shy or too much of a coward, and the words didn't come.

"I don't want you to worry about money," I said, as I cradled her in my arms after this second round of lovemaking. "That's why I wanted to buy this place. I thought I could make things easier."

"I appreciate that," she said. Her arms wrapped tighter around my chest, as if pulling me into a hug. "But I don't want to sell. I can't let this place out of my family—not yet, anyway."

"But what about your new real estate office?" I asked. Liz had told me all about her and Darcy's plans to expand into the neighboring town. She had even mentioned it might be revenue from the sale of the hardware store that made the new office a reality.

"Don't worry about that," Darcy told me. "Liz and I are doing well. We'll save enough money for it eventually. And it's not going to kill us to wait a little longer to get another office. Especially if I have a big renovation here to worry about."

"I hope it's not a worry," I said. Darcy seemed on board with the idea for the recording studio. I even thought I sensed a bit of excitement in her voice, but I couldn't help double-checking with her. I wanted to make sure she was fully on board. And I wanted her to know that she could still back out of this if she wanted to.

Darcy shifted so she rested on her elbow. It meant she could look up at me, our faces close together.

"Not a worry," she said, shaking her head. "It feels right."

Darcy's eyes cast up to the ceiling, and I saw her take in the walls and the room as if it were a person she was getting a good look at.

"I think my dad would have liked it," she said, and they were the kindest words I had heard in a long time. "This place is ready for a new life. I'm excited for its next chapter."

23

DARCY

"Oh my God, what time is it?" I asked, suddenly noticing how the sun was setting outside the window. Liz was expecting us back at the school!

"The play!" Callum said as his eyes went wide. "I completely forgot!"

We were suddenly scrambling for our clothes, pulling T-shirts and underwear from on top of or between stacks of papers around the room. I ran my hands through my hair, desperate for a mirror, as Callum tried to find a missing sock.

"No time," I said, slipping my feet back into my sneakers. "Liz is going to kill us!"

I watched Callum slide his sockless foot into his shoe, and then we were checking each other's clothes and making sure we looked presentable. I rushed out of the office to find my purse and keys, and Callum grabbed his guitar as we rushed out the front door. As I locked the place up, I wondered if I felt something different about the store already. The storefront felt more alive than it had in months, as if the very walls of the store understood there was something exciting on the horizon.

"She called me three times!" Callum said as he checked his phone. I knew my phone would have similar missed calls from Liz. Instead of checking, I rushed toward my car and told Callum to text her we were on our way.

#

"Where were you?" Liz whispered as Callum and I slid our way into the open seats. Someone was on the stage giving a speech about how hard all the kids had worked this week at camp and asking us to turn off our cell phones. I glanced at Liz but said nothing. The smile she gave me seemed to say she knew exactly where we had been, and I felt my cheeks flush when she looked at me like that.

"We lost track of time," I whispered back. Callum settled into his seat, and I took my place on a folding chair in between him and Liz.

"I bet you did," Liz mumbled. The lights went down then, making me lose sight of Liz's expression, and then the torn, red curtain opened with a jerk to reveal a group of kids dressed as jungle animals. The parents and grandparents "oohed" and "awwed" as they saw their kids up on stage. Liz's youngest, Maggie, was front and center, taking the song far too seriously. We laughed as she nearly hit the child next to her with her aggressive choreography.

"She's so cute!" Callum whispered to me. As he leaned into me, his hand reached over to squeeze my leg right above the knee. It was an easy, casual gesture, as if he had done it a hundred times before. It made me smile as I felt a rush of joy in the moment. Everything felt surprisingly *right*. I was sitting with my best friend and a man who cared about me.

I reached down to the hand that still rested casually on

my knee, and I took Callum's hand in my own. He squeezed it in a warm gesture, and we turned our attention to the kids on the stage. We sat hand in hand as a parade of different animal groups crossed the stage. I spent the play searching for Liz's kids on the stage and catching Callum's expressions out of the corner of my eye. He was beaming as he watched his niece and nephew perform.

"I don't want to miss this," he whispered, and at first I didn't understand what he was saying, but he continued. "I don't want to miss them growing up."

I squeezed his hand in response as the last note of the song was pounded out on the out-of-tune piano. The kids finished the song with their arms over their heads and we all clapped our hands in appreciation, wanting nothing more than to make them feel special. The lights around us came up as the kids shuffled their way off and that hiccupping curtain slid back across the auditorium stage.

"That's intermission," Liz said. "I have to get to the concessions table!"

Liz pushed her way out of the aisle, unable to wait for the people in front of her to wander out on their own. It left me and Callum alone, feeling slightly lost in a sea of parents and elementary-school-aged children.

"Should we help her?" I asked. Callum nodded.

"It's the least we can do after being late."

"We weren't late!" I corrected. "We got here just in time."

I shuffled our way out of the row, stepping around people's knees as they looked through the program that had been printed on someone's home printer.

"Even if we had been late," Callum said, leaning into me so he was speaking to the back of my neck. "It would have been worth it."

I felt my body flush with the memory of our time in the

office. I wanted to turn around and kiss him, and if it weren't for all the kids running around, I probably would have done so. Instead, I had to be content to take his hand and guide him to the snacks where Liz was manning the cash box. I saw Liz's eyes drop from our faces to my hand that held tight to Callum's.

"Good show, huh?" She asked.

"They're so adorable!" I squealed. Liz made change for a twenty and handed it to the man in front of her as Callum and I gushed about her children and their performance onstage.

"They must get their talent from their uncle," Callum said, teasing his sister. Liz shoved her shoulder into his as she counted the snacks the mom in front of her was buying. We were now standing behind the table with her, helping people pick out the bake-sale snacks they wanted.

"Did you forget about my stint in that a cappella group?" Liz asked. "The school newspaper said we were 'radiant'."

I snorted as the memory came back to me.

"Didn't we join that group because you had some crush on a boy?" I asked, but Liz quickly corrected me.

"It was *you* who had a crush!" she laughed. "You went on and on about Darren Sykes for weeks until I finally got tired of you not *doing* anything, and I signed us up for his a cappella group."

"And what happened?" Callum asked. "Was it a true-love connection?" He raised his eyebrows in mock interest, as if it were very important to know if this relationship worked out between us.

"We quickly realized Darren Sykes had no interest in me, though Liz did her best to push us together any chance she got," I laughed. "Until we found out his boyfriend sang in the tenor section!"

I looked up at Callum, expecting to see a laugh spreading across his face, but he seemed disconnected, as if he hadn't heard my story. Instead, his eyes were scanning the sea of people filling the auditorium. He looked slightly panicked, as if he had just caught sight of a ghost.

"Are you alright?" I asked.

"Yeah," he said. "Sorry—I just saw someone who looked familiar."

In a town of a few thousand people, the chances of seeing familiar faces at the summer camp play were high. But I had to remind myself that Callum was only recently back in town. There were bound to be tons of people he hadn't run into yet, and each new face could inspire a flood of memories for him.

"Callum Jones!" We heard in front of us. "Can I have your autograph?"

We glanced over to a middle-aged man holding out a napkin he had just picked up from the snack table. I was standing close enough to Callum to feel his body stiffen as he took in the man's request. The evening had felt so normal, but I realized all at once that normal evenings were few and far between when you were Callum Jones.

"Why don't we leave the autographs to the kids tonight?" Callum suggested, and a few of the parents around him chuckled in appreciation.

"It's just an autograph, man," the guy said. He continued to hold the napkin out and now he was pushing it even closer to Callum's chest. It made me uncomfortable, and I wanted to push the man's hands away from him and tell him to leave us alone. I looked up at Callum to see if he would appreciate my help, but his eyes were once again scanning the room. He seemed to catch sight of someone, and I read shock on his face once more.

"If you'll excuse me," Callum said, and then he was squeezing past me so he no longer stood behind the snack table. Liz and I shared a look as we tried to figure out what Callum was doing. As Liz took the next payment from the woman in front of her, I watched Callum cross the room and lock eyes with a short man with spiky hair dyed far too blond.

"Who's that?" I asked, nodding over at the man, but Liz couldn't look up. She was too absorbed in counting out the quarters that had just been handed to her.

I watched as Callum's face grew dark and saw confusion in his features as he spoke with the man. I was too far away to hear anything, but they looked like they were arguing. I felt unease settle into my stomach and tighten the muscles along my shoulder blades. I didn't like the look of things, and I suddenly wanted to be over there, protecting Callum from whatever unpleasantness was in front of him.

"Be right back," I mumbled to Liz. There were plenty of moms behind the snack table, so it wasn't a problem for me to leave. I locked eyes on Callum and the blond man and wove in and out of the people. I pushed my way past bouquets of supermarket flowers parents held in their arms, ready to give to their kids after the show, and I narrowly avoided cups of fruit punch and orange soda that others held, likely wishing it was alcohol.

But by the time I got to the spot where Callum and the man were standing, they were gone. I looked around and caught sight of them at the edge of the room and then saw Callum press against the crash bar on the door and push his way out, this man following behind him. I knew I should leave them alone. I told myself it was probably a private conversation and I shouldn't get myself involved, but I couldn't shake the feeling that this guy was bad news.

Even though I knew Callum could handle himself, I didn't want him to be alone. I made the quick decision to go after them and, before I knew it, I was weaving through more gifts and oversized cameras on my way toward the door.

24

CALLUM

"You didn't answer my calls!"

I stood outside in the school parking lot, my manager across from me. Brady had his hands on his hips as he spoke to me. He had recently acquired a lip ring that made him look like a high school drug dealer instead of the rock star I'm sure he wanted to look like.

"So, you show up here?" I asked. Seeing him in the auditorium had been a shock to the system. At first, I didn't think it was him. Well, I *hoped* it wasn't him. But not many people in the town had bleach-blond hair and a penchant for leather jackets in the summer. Even now, I couldn't believe he wasn't sweating underneath all those layers of clothes.

"It was important I talk to you," Brady explained. "I know you're *taking a break* or whatever you're calling it, but I'm getting concerned."

"You don't have to worry about me. I'm fine."

"Sure, *you're* fine. But what about the band? All of these rumors about a solo career are really hurting us, man."

"I didn't start those rumors!" It was frustrating to have this conversation with him when we had already talked about it. But I knew this defensiveness was also hiding the truth of what I was planning. If I stayed in town and opened this recording studio, then my life with the Horizon would change. And I couldn't forget that moment in the hardware store when I finally admitted to Darcy just how much I wanted to write and record my own album.

"Well, you're not doing much to dispute them," Brady accused. He had a way of stating things as fact even when they were only half true. It had always driven me crazy, and I felt anger surging through me as I heard this.

"What are you talking about? I had the PR team write me a statement. We put it out on social media!"

"And the radio interview?"

The words stopped me. Had Brady heard it? I thought back to everything I had said. It had started out fine—I told them I was fully committed to the band. And I had stuck to the script my team had given me. But then there was the stuff about enjoying my time at home, and the recording studio ...

"I said what they told me to," I deflected. I didn't know exactly what Brady was talking about yet, and I wasn't about to throw myself under the bus.

"Oh really?" he asked, his voice incredulous. "They told you to talk about a whole new business venture? They approved you to tell the world you're going to open a recording studio in this tiny town?"

"The *world*?" I shot back. "It's a small-town radio station! How did you even hear it?"

"That's my job," Brady answered. "And it's not the point. I came here to ask you: Are you committed to the Horizon or not?"

The words were angry and felt too loud in the quiet summer night around us. I could only blink at him as I tried to think of what I could say. Of course, I cared for the band and my bandmates. And I was incredibly proud of the music we had made together. The thought of leaving the band entirely was painful. That wasn't what I wanted.

"Of course I'm committed," I said, lowering my voice to the level of regular conversation. If I was going to explain myself, I needed to be rational. I could only hope Brady would respond in kind. "The band means everything to me. And those guys are my closest friends. I don't want to leave the band."

"Well, it's nice to hear you say that." Brady nodded. "I'm going to need you to say it more often. *And* on social media. We need to fix things before this next tour."

"Wait," I stopped him before he could dive into whatever plans he had for our next publicity ventures. His eyes narrowed at me when he heard this, as if he knew he shouldn't have trusted me.

"You know I don't have time for waiting," Brady shot back. I almost laughed at it—it was such a strange thing to say, but it was exactly something I would expect out of my manager.

"I'm committed to the Horizon, but things can't stay the same forever," I continued. "I've been interested in doing my own album for a long time. And if I'm going to remain creative and keep writing, then I need to try out some new things. Just because I want to work on something new doesn't mean I need to leave the band."

"And this recording studio?" he asked. His voice was dripping with disdain for the idea. I knew in an instant what Brady thought of it and, by extension, what he thought of me.

"You don't think I can do it," I said. It was like I was seeing Brady for the first time. Or I finally stopped ignoring all the red flags that made him such an unlikeable person.

"Hey, now." He put his hands up as if I were about to hit him. "I never said that."

"You didn't have to, Brady. I can tell what you think of me. Some rock star who can't take care of himself and doesn't understand the business. Well, that might have been the case when I was nineteen, but I'm in my thirties now. And it's time for me to make some decisions about my own life."

"Whoa, whoa!" he cried. "No one's stopping you from living a life. I'm just reminding you about your responsibilities. Things are going well for us—it's not the time to shake that up."

"You mean it's not the time to shake up your bank account!"

The words were harsh, and I regretted them as soon as I said them. But on some level, I knew they were true. Brady had a few other clients, most of them acquired after the success of the Horizon, but we were his biggest moneymakers. And I knew the sort of lavish lifestyle he led and likely wanted to maintain. If we were touring less or making fewer appearances on TV shows, it would affect Brady's lifestyle most of all. My bandmates and I certainly had enough money to keep us going for a while even if we took a full year off.

"Is that what you think of me?" Brady asked. I thought he might get mad, instead he played the victim. He looked at me with a pained expression, as if I had just broken up with him. "I hope you realize how committed I've been to this band. I've sacrificed my own life to make sure you all were successful."

"That's the problem," I said, keeping my own voice cool

and calm. "No one should be sacrificing everything. We can do this without losing sight of our families and our friends. We can leave space for people to explore other interests!"

"I didn't think we would come to this," Brady said. He was shaking his head, putting on a big show of looking upset. "I really didn't want to have this conversation with you."

"Brady, I think we should get the band together. Let's talk about making this work. I'm not leaving, I just want a less grueling tour schedule. I think some of the other guys will agree."

"I've talked to the other guys. Frankly, they're quite upset you haven't come to them to have this conversation."

Was this true? I thought about my bandmates and wondered if they would really confide in Brady before they confided in me. I hadn't talked to anyone since coming home except for a brief phone call with Liam after my concert in town. Was that proof they were upset with me? It wasn't like them to stay silent about things like that. We had always been open with each other.

"I'll talk to them," I offered.

"Too late for that."

"What do you mean it's too late?"

"We had a band meeting last night."

"You had a band meeting without me?" I cried. This made me angry, and I couldn't help the way my voice raised in frustration.

"I needed to know how they were feeling. And besides, it's not like you've been easy to reach these days. You've ignored my texts! We talked about the future and all the things you've said in public about settling down and putting down roots."

"You're taking my words out of context," I said. "You should let me explain myself."

Brady barreled forward, ignoring my words.

"The other guys are committed to the band. They know it still has more to achieve, and they need a lead singer who's as passionate and committed as they are."

"Why are you speaking for them?" I asked. I felt a sense of betrayal surging up inside of me. The guys in my band were like family to me. It was wrong for Brady to be here, telling me what they thought about all of this. If they were so upset, why hadn't they told me?

"We need commitment from you. And if you're not willing to commit, then it might be time to pursue other options."

The words made my whole body go cold. I stared back at him, my face neutral.

"And what does that mean?" I asked.

"It's been done before—in some ways the lead singer is the easiest guy to replace."

"You want to replace me?" It was something I had never expected, and the shock of this made rage surge through me. I squeezed my fists hard beside me as I fought an urge to punch the brick wall we stood next to. "I write all our music! I'm the face of the whole band!"

"That's right," Brady nodded. "Which is why we need someone fully dedicated to the band. We can't have you writing all the good songs for yourself and this solo album and then giving the Horizon all the scraps."

"You really think I would do that?" I asked. "You really think I would actively *hurt* the band I created? We built this thing up from our college dorm rooms. It's not something I can just throw away."

"Isn't that what you're doing?" Brady asked. "I came here

to find out if you're committed to this thing. And to tell you that if you're not one hundred percent in, then we're prepared to find someone who is."

I couldn't speak. I had no words as Brady stood there, offering me an ultimatum. Could this actually happen? Could the band cut me out of the group I had created? Were they really willing to pull some random guy off the street and put him front and center singing all of my songs? It was too much to fathom. I didn't want to give up the Horizon. That had never been my intention, and I felt helpless as Brady stood in front of me, taking the choice away from me.

"You can't do that," I protested. "You can't just kick me out."

"You're only one person in a group of four," Brady told me, his voice cold and calculating. "All it takes is the votes."

Was this true? I had never thought about the legal side of the band or my own rights as a creator of it. Were there laws outlining these things? Did we have a contract between bandmates that said this sort of thing? I thought back to the long documents I signed all those years ago when Brady became our manager. Had I signed away my rights to my own band? Did we give him this power?

"I don't want to leave," I said carefully. I felt like I was walking on a tightrope. One wrong step and I would fall to my death. It made my voice tight and my muscles taut as if I were frozen in place.

"That's good to hear," he said. Brady had all the power right now, and he knew it. He seemed smug, as if some part of him was enjoying this. "We've had an offer for a summer tour. A band dropped out and they need a replacement. You leave in a week."

"A week?" I asked. My mind flew to all the plans I had made with Liz and my promise to my niece and nephew that we would go to the theme park Liz and I had loved as kids. And then there was Darcy. I saw her in the hardware store, the sun setting behind her as she watched me sing. I saw the care and admiration on her face and the way she listened to every word. It was just the two of us and nothing else to worry about. I wanted more of that.

"If you can't do it, I'm sure we can find someone else."

"Someone else?" I asked, my voice full of skepticism. "Who are you going to find on a week's notice?"

"Liam knows all the music," Brady said with a nonchalance that made me want to scream. "Maybe it's time he got promoted from backup vocals to our lead singer."

25

DARCY

Just as I thought I was working my way through the crowd, the lights in the auditorium flashed, telling the parents the second half was about to begin. Now I was pushing my way through a sea of people trying to move in the opposite direction.

"Excuse me," I said each time I bumped into another eager aunt or uncle. People groaned at me or rolled their eyes as I elbowed my way toward the door. Callum had left with that strange man, and I suddenly felt panicked that he might simply get in his car and disappear.

Stop being ridiculous, I told myself, but something about Callum and that blond man was making me uneasy. I needed to get out there and hear what they were saying.

Finally, I made my way out of the crowd and had a clear path to the door. In front of me I saw the double doors that led to the elementary school hallway, but there was another door to my right that seemed to lead outside. I couldn't remember which door Callum and the man had taken. Unwilling to risk setting off some fire alarm by pushing through the door to my right, I pushed out into the hallway. I looked left and right, but Callum wasn't there.

They must have gone outside.

I turned toward the front entrance of the school as my mind raced with possibilities. Who was that man and what were they talking about? I left the front entrance and turned to my right. I figured I could walk around the outside of the building to get to where Callum and this man were likely talking. If they were still here, that is. I had a quick pang of guilt as I thought of Liz sitting down for the second half of the play with two empty seats next to her, but I reasoned she would approve of my quest. She was a big supporter of Callum and me being together and here I was, trying to make sure he wasn't in any trouble.

"You haven't left us any other options."

I heard the voices floating to me as I neared the auditorium. This portion of the building seemed to be an add-on, and it jutted out from the original portion of the building. It meant that, as I walked toward them, I couldn't be seen, but I could hear them clearly only a few feet away from me.

"And the other guys are on board with this?" Callum's voice sounded strained and a bit frantic. I sensed panic in his voice, and I knew for sure something was wrong.

"I told you they all decided. They need someone dedicated to what we're doing. Someone who cares."

"Seriously?" The accusation made me mad, and it wasn't even directed at me. I could only imagine what Callum was feeling. "You're telling me I'm not serious? When I've sacrificed everything to make that group successful!"

"You used to," the man said. I had a vague recollection of Callum telling me about his manager, a man he didn't like much. "But you've made it very clear your priorities have changed."

"Because I want to spend time with my family? Because I don't want to be in a new city every single night getting barely any sleep between stops?"

"You knew what you were signing up for," the man said. "When we first started all of this, I told you I would take you to the top. I tried to prepare you for it."

"Oh, *you* took us to the top?" Callum's voice was dripping with disdain. I could hear him struggling to keep control. It reminded me of his confrontation with my ex. I could only hope this argument wouldn't end in a black eye like that one had. "We should have dropped you years ago, Brady! We're the only successful band you've ever had."

"Wow, how conceited can you get?" Brady fired back. "You're a big client, Callum, but I have plenty of other work to keep me busy. If you don't like my work, then why don't you talk to your bandmates about it? I can tell you with certainty they have no problem with the way I'm managing this band. In fact, they're the ones who told me to come here. They know this tour is a great opportunity for you all, and they wanted me to convince you."

A tour?

"They all want to do this?" Callum asked. I sensed hesitation in his voice, as if he couldn't tell what was true and what was false. He sounded vulnerable, and part of me wanted to go to him. But the words of his manager kept me in place. Was Callum going back on the road? Was he about to leave after everything we had just talked about?

"They're all on board," Brady assured him. "And when you hear what they're offering you, you'll understand why. This tour is a big deal. And there's even more money because it's so last-minute. I wouldn't come here if I didn't think it was the right move for the group."

"Couldn't we join the tour late?" Callum asked. "We could go right after the summer."

"They don't want two replacements. They want one," Brady said. "The tour dates are booked. Sold out arenas all over the country."

There was silence then. I took the risk of leaning out just enough to get a glimpse of Callum and the man standing with him. I could see the blond man's back, but Callum's face was there, looking pained and confused. He cast his eyes up to the sky and ran his hand through his hair.

"I can't do it, Brady. I have plans with my family and ... I can't just drop everything and leave."

"Then Liam will do it."

The words were shockingly final. Brady said them quickly and definitively with no room for conversation.

"No way!" Callum cried out. "He doesn't have the voice for that. They're *my* songs!"

"You're wrong there," Brady said, spitting back in disgust. "Those songs belong to the band and the record labels who recorded them. And if you try to take a single one with you for this new *solo career* you're planning, then we'll sue you. You can be sure of that."

"This is ridiculous! You can't shove me out of my own band."

"Who's shoving you out? *You're* the one saying no! *You're* the one refusing to put your career and this band before the other things in your life."

I saw Brady step away, as if he were about to head back to his car. Callum reached out in desperation and grabbed his arm.

"Wait! Don't do this—just let me think. You're putting me in a horrible situation."

"I don't have time to wait. We're doing this tour with or without you. So, are you in or are you out?"

"Let me talk about it with my sister. I need a bit of time to see if this can work."

But Brady was pulling away again. He crossed to the parking lot and Callum followed him, both walking closer to where I was hiding behind the corner of the building.

"I'm calling the band," Brady said as he walked. "I'll tell Liam to get ready. We already have a sub bass player lined up. He's already started learning the songs."

"Stop!" Callum cried out, his voice pleading. Finally, Brady stood still and turned back to him. It was as if he knew he had won, and my heart sank into my toes. There was a confidence in that spin that made me want to shove the man down to the ground.

Don't say it, I begged him. *Please don't say it.*

"Don't call Liam," Callum said. "Tell them I'll do the tour. Tell them I'm in."

Disappointment flooded through me and brought tears instantly to my eyes. He was leaving. After all his plans at the hardware store and all those caring words to me, he was choosing to leave. I wanted to kick myself for trusting him. I wanted to scream and yell for letting myself fall victim to Callum Jones when he had shown me time and time again that he shouldn't be trusted.

"Perfect," Brady said with a smug smile, but just then he caught sight of me from the corner of his eye. And then both men looked over at me. Callum's mouth fell open as he realized I had heard their conversation. He took a step forward, but my vision was suddenly blurred by tears that overflowed, falling down my cheeks. I was ashamed to cry in front of him. I felt stupid and small and overwhelmed by the feeling Callum had tricked me into something.

"Darcy," Callum called out, but I rushed away from him. I couldn't face him like this, and I knew I wouldn't be able to have a rational conversation. Right now, I needed to get away from him.

"Leave me alone," I yelled as I walked to the parking lot. I fished through my bag to find my keys, telling myself to stop crying. But the tears kept coming.

He never promised you anything, I told myself. *He never said he would stay.*

I had taken all his talk about the recording studio and his plans for the future as a commitment to me, but had Callum ever said that? Had he ever told me he wanted a relationship with me? I felt more and more stupid as I reached my car and finally located my keys.

"I had to tell him that," Callum said, keeping his voice low. He was next to me now, watching as I unlocked my car and opened the door. "I just needed everything to slow down for a minute so I could think!"

"It's fine," I told him, forcing myself to look at him. "I always knew you were going back on the road. You don't owe me anything."

"Don't say that!" Callum said. "Just give me a minute."

But I couldn't stand there. I got in the car and slammed the door before shoving the keys into the ignition. I backed up too quickly—lucky there were no cars behind me—and then turned hard to head out of the parking lot. Callum stood there, his arms limp by his sides, looking defeated as I drove away.

26

CALLUM

I thought about going back inside to say goodbye to Liz. She was going to be very confused when neither Darcy nor I came back inside to watch the performance. But then I thought about trying to fight my way through rows of audience members so I could whisper an explanation to her. It would be far too disruptive.

Instead, I sent her a text as I sought out my car in the parking lot.

Something came up. Everyone's fine but we had to leave.

It was a strange message, but I couldn't think of any other way to say it. Not without typing a whole paragraph of explanation. I looked down at the text and then added:

I'll call you soon.

I hoped it was enough to put Liz's mind at ease. With that taken care of, I turned on the engine and backed my car out of the parking space. Brady was still pacing back and forth in front of the school, his cell phone glued to his ear. He was probably on the phone with the band already, telling them he had succeeded in his mission. It made me sick to think he might already be putting the wheels in motion for this summer tour.

But I didn't have time to think about that. First, I needed to find Darcy. I would deal with Brady and the band once I had a chance to talk to her. But as I pulled out of the school parking lot, I realized I had no idea where Darcy had gone. The immediate places that came to mind included her house, the real estate office, and the hardware store.

Since I was close to Main Street, I set off toward the hardware store and her office that was just down the street. Though I knew she wouldn't answer, I tried calling her. I even left a voicemail.

"Darcy. It's not what you think. Please let me know where you are so we can talk about this. I promise I can explain."

I paused then, wondering if I should say more, but I simply hung up, ending the message. I texted as well.

Let's talk about this. Please tell me where you are.

It wasn't surprising that I didn't get a response. I could still see her face as she looked at me through the car window, full of hurt and betrayal. I hated Brady in that moment. How could he put me in this situation? And how had he made me agree to something I was so strongly against? I knew I had acted out of fear in the face of Brady's bullying behavior. I gave into him because I was afraid of what would happen if I said no.

But now I could see that saying yes was even worse. I had betrayed Darcy and, what was even worse, I had betrayed myself. When I really thought about it, I had wanted to take a break from the band for a long time and it was time for me to recognize this.

"Darcy? Are you in there?"

I knocked on the door of the hardware store, attempting

to peer through the windows. It was dark inside, and the door was locked tight. I knocked louder, just in case she was inside.

"Can we please talk?"

A man on the sidewalk looked up at me and I could tell he was uncomfortable by my behavior. He seemed uncertain if he should intervene in whatever situation he had come across.

"It's alright," I said, turning to him. "I'm leaving."

I walked past the man and slammed back into my car. His eyes were on me as I did a U-turn on the narrow street and took off toward the real estate office.

But she wasn't there either. Once again I was met with a quiet and locked building.

Darcy ... where are you?

Just as I asked myself the question, I heard a chime from my phone. I rushed to pull it from my pocket and my heart nearly skipped a beat as I saw Darcy's name flash across it.

No need to explain. I shouldn't be surprised. Ever since we were teenagers, you've been doing this. As soon as I get close you pull away. You did it at seventeen and I'm not surprised you're doing it now. Enjoy your tour.

The finality of these words and the clear judgment against me and my past actions was a sharp pain in my chest. Darcy was angry. That I understood. But her words seemed to imply that I was somehow tricking her or hurting her on purpose. That was painful to me. And worse, she thought this was some pattern of behavior, something I had done in the past. *Ever since we were teenagers ...*

I thought back to our date all those years ago. What did Darcy mean? I was the one who had been left all those years ago. She disappeared without a word before I had a chance to show her how much she meant to me. A question gnawed at me, and I thought about the outdoor amphitheater where we had our first date. A local band we both liked had been playing.

I stood on the sidewalk outside of Darcy and Liz's real estate office and wondered what to do next. Should I text back? The message was so final. It didn't feel like we could have a productive conversation if we weren't face-to-face. That concert kept floating back into my head... if Darcy was thinking about that place, could she have gone there?

Running on pure instinct, I rushed back to my car. I knew it was crazy. It was dumb to think Darcy had gone to the site of our first date. And yet, I couldn't shake the feeling that this was what everything had been leading to. This was the unspoken thing that hung between us after all these years. And it was time to face it.

I rushed to the amphitheater with my heart pounding in my chest. I felt nervous, worried what she would do when she saw me. I feared she had already decided and wouldn't be willing to talk to me.

The phone rang next to me and I rushed to answer it, only to see it was Liz's name that popped up on the screen.

"What the hell?" she asked. "You just disappeared."

"Sorry." I took a hard right onto a dirt road, feeling my tires bump over the uneven surface. "I texted you, though. Everyone's fine."

"Everyone except your niece and nephew! They asked about you the second they got off the stage."

I realized all at once that I had forgotten about Maggie and Alan who had spent the past week talking about how excited they were for me to see their performance.

"God, Liz, I'm so sorry. Tell them I'll make it up to them. Do you want to put them on?"

"They're distracted by the ice cream sundae bar we've set

up to celebrate the end of camp. But you'll definitely have some explaining to do when you're home tonight. What's going on?"

"Brady showed up."

"Your *manager* Brady?"

"Exactly. And he tried to blackmail me into going back on tour early. He said he was going to kick me out of the band and let Liam sing all the songs."

"Liam?" I was comforted by the shock in Liz's voice. "He thinks *Liam* can be the lead singer? He can barely keep rhythm when he's on backup vocals."

"Thank you!" I cried out. It was comforting to hear someone else voicing the same opinions I had. For what felt like the hundredth time this summer, I felt grateful to have Liz in my corner.

"So what does this have to do with Darcy?" Liz asked. "Are you leaving?"

"No!" I cried out, but then I had to stop myself. "Well, I sort of told Brady I was. And Darcy overheard me. But I don't actually want to go!"

"And yet you told him you would?"

Liz was skeptical on the other end of the phone, and I knew she wasn't wrong. Instead of being an adult and voicing what I wanted, I had let Brady influence me into saying what he wanted to hear.

"I know. It was a mistake. But I didn't know Darcy was there. I thought I could tell him yes just to get the guy out of my face. And then I would figure out how to work it all out."

"And instead you made an even bigger mess of things."

"You're not wrong."

I sighed as I caught sight of the amphitheater out in the park. The open field looked empty, but there were a handful of cars in the parking lot. Though evening was falling, the sky was still bright on this summer evening, and people were enjoying the extended daylight out in the park. I scanned the cars quickly and there, sitting a few spaces away from me, was Darcy's car.

"Liz, I have to go. I'm trying to fix things."

"Just be honest, Callum. Lying and trying to say what other people want to hear will only get you into trouble. If you want to go back out on tour, tell Darcy that. And if you want to stay, you know my door is always open."

"Thanks, Liz." Her words were exactly what I needed to hear. She was giving me permission to think about what I wanted, and I knew that whatever decision I made, my sister would support me.

"Call me later."

I hung up the phone and looked down toward the outdoor stage. The parking lot sat on a hill and the amphitheater was below, allowing people to set up blankets on the hill to watch whatever performance was showing. I strained my eyes and thought I could see a figure sitting on the edge of the stage. Was it Darcy?

My heart beat fast as I thought about what I would say to her. But I couldn't form exact words. I knew I needed to let the truth emerge when I was with her. It was time to trust myself, and to trust that I would say the right thing when the moment came.

27

DARCY

I saw him when he was still a few hundred yards away. After thinking about him all afternoon, it was surprising to see him actually walking toward me as the fireflies popped out across the field. I could have left. It would have been easy to get up and leave, closing the door forever. But I stayed where I was. I couldn't help thinking that Callum had just passed a test I didn't know I was setting for him.

He had found me. And now we were back to the very beginning of our relationship, where everything had started and also ended.

"What are you doing here?"

The words were out of me as soon as he was in earshot. I knew it wasn't the kindest thing to say, but something in me still wanted to push him away. It was like I was still giving him the chance to leave.

Callum didn't respond right away. He just continued to walk toward me, alternating between looking at me and watching his feet as they walked through the grass and navigated uneven ground. When he was close to me, he gave me a slight smile.

"Hey," he said. I was sitting with my legs over the edge of the stage, kicking my heels against the wood along the front. Callum took a seat next to me so we were both staring at the ground rather than looking at each other.

"How did you find me?"

"I didn't at first. I checked the hardware store and your office. But then you texted ..."

I was already feeling uncomfortable about the text I had sent him. I had meant it as a final communication between us, a last goodbye of sorts. But now he was here, talking to me. I realized how cowardly I was being, running away from this important conversation.

"Sorry about that," I mumbled. "I should have stayed to talk to you."

"I get it," he said, and I felt how he wanted to put me at ease. "I didn't know you were standing there. I wouldn't have said that." I could tell how much he wanted me to listen to him. He spoke quickly, as if he didn't know how much time I would give him to speak.

"I would have heard it eventually," I said. "And honestly, I'm glad I know now."

"But you don't!" he said. "Because *I* don't even know what I'm doing. I don't want to leave."

The words should have brought comfort, but I only felt sadness as I heard how non-committal they were. It only drove home the point that Callum wasn't sure about us. He wasn't ready to make a commitment.

"Do you remember our first date?" I blurted out. It was impossible not to think of this when we were sitting in the very place where the date had taken place. "I was so excited to go out with you. I spent that whole summer telling Liz how cute I thought you were."

"I was thinking the same thing," he laughed. "Though I don't know if I had the courage to tell Liz about it. I think it took the entire summer to get up the courage to ask you out."

I looked over at him, feeling anger rise in my chest as I took in the words. It wasn't right for him to rewrite history now. It wasn't fair for him to pretend he had a crush on me or act like he had any interest in his little sister's friend. I stood up and walked away from him, fighting against an impulse to lash out at him.

Instead, I wrapped my arms around myself and stared up the hill, imagining a fifteen-year-old version of myself nearly buzzing with excitement over going on a date with an older guy who was heading off to college. I remembered how hopeful I had been and all the plans I had made as I dreamed naively about a future with Callum.

"Darcy?" He asked. Callum was next to me, and I couldn't stop myself from turning to face off against him.

"Please don't pretend you were interested in me back then. You can't just make up whatever version of events works for you now."

"What are you talking about?" He seemed taken aback, but I didn't have time to analyze his feelings.

"I already told you in the text. You abandoned me then without a word, so I shouldn't be surprised you were about to do exactly the same thing now. So don't pretend that date was some fairy tale where you got to take out the girl of your dreams. It's just not true!"

"Abandoned you?" Callum looked shocked, as if I had just slapped him across the face.

"You don't remember?" I felt tears prick at my eyes, and I

thought about pushing past him and rushing to my car. It was bad enough what had happened all those years ago, but the thought that Callum didn't even *remember* was even more painful. Especially when I had carried the memory around for so long.

"You *left* me!" I cried out. "I was *so* excited when you came to pick me up. And then we were at the concert with your friends and everything seemed to be going so well. I thought we were actually having a good time!"

My voice was too loud, and I felt too dramatic as I talked about this. It was like my teenage self was back in this field, confronting Callum after years of silence.

"We *were* having a good time," Callum responded, but once again I felt frustration build inside of me as I took in his interpretation of events.

"Clearly not!" I called out, still too loud. "Because next thing I knew you simply *disappeared*. I went off to the bathroom, and when I came back you were gone. I couldn't find you anywhere."

I glared at him then, practically begging him to give me an explanation. That feeling of confusion and hurt when I realized Callum was gone was something I had never been able to let go. I could still remember fighting my way through the crowds with a big smile on my face. I could remember thinking of all the things I wanted to say to Callum after our great conversation all night and how excited I was as I wondered if he would hold my hand or offer me his jacket once it got darker outside.

But when I found our blanket, spread out on the hill, Callum and his friends were gone. His jacket wasn't there anymore, and the small cooler he had packed with drinks and snacks was missing too. In fact, everything was gone except for the blanket itself. I remember standing there, trying to understand what was happening. And I remember looking around and wondering if the people sitting around me had seen it all. Did they know I had been left?

Now, as all those emotions rushed back, I forced myself to stand tall in front of him. I forced myself to stare into his eyes and wait for an explanation. I scanned his face for any sign of remorse, but I only saw confusion and a brief sense of outrage. Was he upset I was confronting him about this after all these years? I gave it another moment, but when he didn't speak, I turned on my heel and walked away from him.

"Darcy!"

Too late, I thought. I kept walking, rushing my way up the hill even though it made my legs burn with the effort.

"Wait! Let me explain!"

I ignored him, setting my sights on the car. I could only think of getting home and slamming the door behind me. I could only think of letting myself fall apart.

"Darcy, please!"

His hand slipped into mine, and he stopped me. I could have pulled away. In fact, I thought about it. But when I looked back at him, I saw there were tears in his eyes. It surprised me, and it was the opening he needed.

"I thought *you* ran away," he said.

I stared at him, unable to do anything except blink. What was he saying? After so many years of obsessing over that night at the concert, it was nearly impossible to imagine a different scenario. Was it all some big misunderstanding? Or was Callum simply telling me what I wanted to hear?

"Just wait," he begged. "Let me explain."

He still held my hand, and I felt him squeeze it slightly, asking me to trust him.

"Alright," I sighed. "Let's talk."

I saw Callum smile as relief flooded his face.

"Okay," he said, his voice light and bouncy. I saw his eyes slide up to his car and then he glanced back at me. "Wait here, okay?"

I felt my eyebrows lift in shock as he asked me to wait. I had just agreed to stay here and talk, and now he was disappearing?

"I know, I know," he said, as if reading my mind. "But just give me a second."

I rolled my eyes, but it seemed to be enough of a "yes" for Callum. He took off at a run toward his car, and I watched as he fished his keys out of his pocket and opened his trunk. I saw a plaid piece of fabric come out before he slammed the trunk closed and rushed back to me. I couldn't help but smile as I realized he was bringing a picnic blanket for us to sit on.

"What's this?" I asked, though of course I knew what it was. Callum stood back and opened the blanket into the air, letting it billow out as he held the corners. He rested it on the grass and invited me to sit down.

"Liz is big on picnics," he laughed. "Or at least she's big on getting me and the kids out of the house for a few hours during lunchtime."

I smiled at this, certain his instincts on Liz and her ulterior motives were entirely correct. He smiled back, and I took him up on his offer to settle onto the blanket. Callum took the spot next to me and I felt the strange tension between us. To anyone in the park, we looked like a happy couple enjoying the final minutes of daytime as the fireflies emerged across the field. They had no way of knowing I saw this, instead, as a potential final goodbye.

28

CALLUM

"So … you were going to tell me about how *I* abandoned *you*?"

Darcy's words were accusatory, and I couldn't blame her. Hearing her talk about how she thought I picked up and left her all those years ago was bringing a whole new understanding to some of the things she had said to me. And it certainly explained her text. I had always thought she *knew* what I tried to do for her all those years ago. But now I wasn't so sure.

"I never knew why you left," I told her. But then I started again. I needed to explain things from the beginning. "I wasn't trying to abandon you. I left because I was going onstage."

"Onstage?" I could tell she was being cautious. She wasn't sure what to believe anymore, and I knew I couldn't blame her for that.

"Do you remember the band? They were a group from town who did lots of covers of the most popular classic rock songs, but they had a few originals here and there. They were only a few years older than me, and they went through our high school."

"I remember," Darcy nodded. "I think they played at my senior prom."

"Probably," I laughed. "The high school was always eager to jump onto their star, even if they were only a mildly successful band playing shows at the local park."

"I take it you're speaking from experience?"

I smiled as Darcy picked up on my annoyance toward the school.

"They call me *every year* to ask me if I want to put my name on the gym or a softball field. It doesn't matter how many times I tell them I hated that place."

"Hated it?" Darcy looked over with a questioning look. "You were always so popular!"

"Really?" For a moment I thought Darcy might be joking. "It certainly never felt that way. I don't think I really understood who I was until I started focusing on music in college and met my bandmates. Popular, huh?"

Darcy shrugged as she looked at me sideways.

"Don't let it go to your head," she mumbled.

We shared a smile, and for a moment I forgot what we were talking about. I wanted to live in the simplicity of that moment. But I forced myself to stay on track.

"Anyway, the band. I knew them a little because they graduated a few years ahead of me. And I had seen enough of their shows around town that they would recognize me and sometimes let me hang out with them."

"So you got caught up saying hello to them? Is that what you're trying to tell me?"

"Not at all," I assured her. "But I did leave to meet up with them."

Darcy looked over at me with a furrowed brow, skepticism clear on her face. I took a deep breath and let it out in a sigh. I was realizing what it meant if Darcy had left when she said she did. It was like the pieces were fitting together to solve a mystery.

"You really left before the band came back? You didn't see them start playing again?"

"No!" Darcy said. I sensed the frustration in her voice. "I came back from the bathroom and saw you had left. And I was way too humiliated to sit on that blanket by myself with everyone staring at me! So I called Liz and walked to the parking lot and then just kept walking. She picked me up at the gas station on the corner."

I shook my head, taking all of this in.

"All this time I thought you knew!" I murmured, more to myself than to her, but Darcy was running out of patience.

"Will you tell me what's going on?"

"I did leave the audience that night, but it wasn't because I didn't like you. Instead, it was because I got up onstage to play a song. I had convinced the band to let me kick off the second half."

"You played that night?"

"Not only that ... I dedicated the song to you."

I could barely look at her when I said this. All of my insecurities about that night were flooding back to me, and I couldn't help but wonder if she was about to reject me again. Would she tell me she actually knew all about it? And that she chose to leave anyway?

"What are you talking about?" I looked up to see a lightness in Darcy's eyes. She was curious to hear about this. I could tell something was warming inside of her, and she was eager to understand the full story. With these few simple words, I was regaining her trust.

"It's true. I'll call up my buddy Justin if you want. Hell,

you can probably ask anyone under the age of thirty in the town. I think everyone heard about it eventually!"

"Except me," Darcy said. "Tell me what happened."

"I had arranged it with the guys that I would kick off after the break. God, I was so nervous. I had barely performed in front of my parents, let alone a crowd of a few hundred people. But I wanted to do it. Mostly because I wanted you to know how I felt. I knew you were younger than me and that I was heading off to college, but even back then I felt a connection between us. Didn't you feel it?"

"Of course I did. That's why I was so hurt when you disappeared."

"God, I should have made Liz come with us. I should have forced her to sit with you so you wouldn't have been left all alone. I didn't think of that!"

"Keep going with the story."

"Sorry. So, I got up there, and I said something about how I had found someone special, and I wanted to dedicate the song to her. I didn't use your name because I thought that might embarrass you too much. But I said that I came here with someone I cared about and that I was looking forward to getting to know our future together. And then I sang. You know the song Summertime Séance? I sang it that night."

"The song from your first album?" She looked over, and I wanted to take her hand. I wanted to feel the connection that had come so naturally when we sat in the auditorium watching the kids perform a show onstage. But even though she was opening up to me, I knew she wasn't quite ready. She still needed to put all the pieces together and then decide if she believed me.

"Yeah, it ended up being the first single for the Horizon.

It was sort of the song that put us on the map." I looked over at her and caught her eye. "I wrote it for you."

"You're lying," she said, and it was the last reaction I expected.

"I'm not!" I found myself laughing as I tried to defend myself. "I wrote that song the summer after high school, right around the time I started realizing how much I enjoyed seeing you around the house when you were hanging with Liz. And around the time you started coming for burgers with my friends or tagging along for the movies. That song is about *you.*"

I could see Darcy thinking about this. I wondered if she was thinking through the lyrics of the song to find any clues. I knew if she listened again she would recognize all the small details of that summer when we were hanging out together.

"So, I dedicated the song to you, and I stood onstage with my guitar and sang that song. I don't think anyone had even heard it yet, because I had only just written it. I was shaking like a leaf the entire time I sang that song!"

"That's why you left," she said, and we both nodded as we realized what a huge misunderstanding that night had been. A misunderstand we had been carrying with us for years. "And then when you came offstage, I wasn't there!"

"Exactly," I said, glad that Darcy understood this next part of the story. "I came offstage beaming, filled with pride that I had done that. And I was *so* excited to come find you. But also very nervous, because I didn't know how you would react. It was still so early in our relationship. Plus you were younger than me, and I was about to head off to college. I was definitely a ball of nerves heading back into that crowd."

"And I was nowhere to be found."

Darcy's voice sounded sad or perhaps disappointed things had turned out this way. I didn't want to rub salt in the wound, but I did want her to understand what I felt.

"I was devastated. I could only imagine that you had heard me say all those things, and you left because you didn't feel the same. It felt like a clear sign that you weren't interested in any type of relationship."

We sat quietly for a moment, both taking in the enormity of the assumptions we had both made that night.

"That's why you said I abandoned you," Darcy said. "You thought I just up and left."

"Exactly. I was mortified. And the last thing I was going to do was call you on the phone or try to talk to you again after you so clearly rejected me. So, I spent the rest of the summer avoiding you. I think I even applied to work in the dining hall just so I could go to school early!"

"And I spent the summer avoiding *you* because I was sure you had ditched me at the concert. And then the next time we saw each other I remember you literally walked in the other direction!"

I laughed at this, but I didn't discount her memory.

"I'm not surprised," I chuckled. "I didn't have very practiced social skills at that time. I probably wasn't subtle."

"You weren't! I guess we ended up just reinforcing each other's fears. I thought you didn't like me, and you thought I had rejected you. And we both avoided any conversations about it."

"We were teenagers!" I offered. "What do you expect?"

"I don't know that it's only a teenager problem," Darcy said. She shifted on the blanket so she could turn her body to face me. "I'm still having trouble telling you what I'm feeling."

"Wait. Before you say anything, I want to talk first."

I thought for a moment Darcy would protest, but then she folded her hands in her lap and raised her eyebrows at me, showing a picture-perfect image of waiting for me to speak. But the second she did this, I felt nerves overtake me. I took a deep breath and pressed forward.

"I'm sorry you overheard my conversation with Brady. I didn't know you were there. But it's no excuse. I should never had said that to him. I should have never told him I would go on the tour."

"You don't owe me anything ..." she started, but I pushed forward, wanting her to understand something. And, in fact, I needed myself to understand it as well.

"I'm not going on tour. I don't *want* to go on tour. I want to stay here."

"But you told him you're going."

"I know. It was a dumb thing to do. But he was standing there telling me he was going to *replace* me. In my own band where I write all the music! He's going to move Liam up front and have him be lead singer."

"Well, that will never work," Darcy said, letting out a little scoff. Her immediate response to this plan made me feel vindicated just as my conversation with Liz had done.

"That's what I tried to say," I agreed. "But he wouldn't listen. And I just wanted some time to think without Brady berating me and telling me I'm not dedicated to the band. It seemed like the easiest thing to say to get him off my back. I just needed time to think."

"So, you want to stay?" Her tone was tentative, and I hated the vulnerability I heard there. I grabbed her hand.

"Darcy, I've never stopped thinking about you. Ever since I was seventeen years old, I've wanted to be with you. So I'm not going anywhere. Even if it means getting kicked out of the very band I created."

I leaned in and kissed her, and I felt Darcy open up to me. She relaxed against me, and after our kiss I felt her arms wrap around me. We hugged each other close, finally seeming to understand each other.

"You can't give up your band," she said into my ear. "I wouldn't ask you to do that."

"You might not, but Liz certainly will. I promised her a full summer, and she's going to hold me to that!" We laughed about Liz and I leaned back from the hug. I took both her hands in mine so I could look at her.

"I'll figure things out with Brady and the band. I've been ready for something to change for a long time. And I'm excited to figure out what that looks like."

"Good," Darcy smiled. "Because we have a solo album to record at your new recording studio."

"You're still up for it?" I hadn't dared to hope she was still interested.

"As long as you promise me you won't leave before it's done, I'm open to it."

"Hmmm ... leaving before something's over? I think *you're* the one we might have to worry about."

Darcy playfully pushed me, and I allowed myself to fall backward as we both laughed. She leaned over and laid her body on top of mine before dropping to kiss me again.

"I won't leave," I told her, staring up into her eyes. "I want to stay here and get to know you better. And I have a feeling that truly knowing Darcy Stevens will take much longer than one summer."

29

DARCY

My mind swirled with all this new information. My body flushed with happiness as I kissed Callum, feeling the solid form of his body beneath me. The fifteen-year-old me would not believe that I was lying in this field with Callum Jones. And to think that our separation all these years was because of some big misunderstanding.

Callum lifted his hand and brushed my hair behind my ear.

"I can't believe we're here," he said, mirroring my own thoughts.

"Me neither. I doubt Liz is going to be too happy with us ... we sort of bailed on the play."

Callum laughed.

"Don't worry, she already gave me an earful. I think I'll have to bring the kids to that theme park I promised them sooner rather than later."

"Can I come?" I asked, feeling like a little kid myself. "I love rollercoasters."

"I knew I liked you," he said with a huge smile.

I bent down and kissed him again, and this time his tongue slid into my mouth. Callum pulled me closer to him, and I pressed my mouth harder against his as the kiss deepened. Our kissing got more intense, filled with desperation and passion fueled by our recent recommitment to one another. I wanted to feel even closer to Callum, and I slid my leg across his body before sliding to be fully on top of him.

"Wait," he said, breaking off the kiss. "There's something I need to do."

I groaned and dropped my head to Callum's chest.

"Now?" I asked with a smile.

"Yes, now." He laughed. He helped guide me off of him and slid up to a seated position so we both sat on the blanket. I saw Callum pull his cell phone out of his pocket. There was a moment of hesitation and I caught him as he glanced over at me. But then he was back to his phone.

"You don't have to worry about Liz," I told him. "You know she'll always forgive her big brother."

Callum put the phone to his ear and gently shook his head at my words.

"Hey. Brady."

I held back a small gasp as I heard the greeting. I looked over at him, trying to catch his eye, but Callum wouldn't look at me.

"You don't have to do this right now ..." I tried, but Callum wasn't listening to me. I was about to try again, but I stopped myself. I realized this phone call wasn't all about me. It was the culmination of what Callum had been thinking about all summer. It was Callum finally speaking his mind and saying what he wanted.

"Listen, I'm not going on tour."

I couldn't hear Brady's words on the other end of the

line, but I could hear a muffled voice. It sounded angry and loud.

"I know that's not what you want to hear, but it's time you realize that I'm a person and not a *product*. Look, I'm grateful for what you've done for the band, but our success is not because of you."

Again, the angry voice. I slid myself closer to Callum and rested a hand on his back, providing comfort.

"Yes, I know how much time you've spent promoting the band and representing us. But it's nothing compared to the hours we spend writing music and practicing and traveling from city to city. So, when we say we need a break, you're going to listen to us. And when the band agrees to something like my summer away, you're not going to turn around and convince them otherwise.

"Just stop talking for a minute! I need you to know that I won't allow you to kick me out of this band. If I need to get lawyers involved, I won't hesitate to do that. So, I think you better call up that company and tell them the Horizon will not be a replacement band on anyone's tour!"

I wanted to cheer as I heard the words, but I knew it wouldn't help Callum if I was overheard. A smile spread wide across my face and I felt giddy with happiness.

"Here's what's going to happen, Brady. I'm not going to hear from you for a month. You're going to sit back and collect your paycheck and forget that the Horizon is even a client for this month. Then, when I'm ready, I'm going to call you and you're going to answer. We'll discuss my solo album and we'll plan the recording of my new music in conjunction with events for the Horizon. And if you don't like this plan, then I think it's time for the Horizon to look for a new manager."

I celebrated silently next to Callum, even grabbing his

shoulders to shake him in pride and appreciation. Callum smiled over at me as he brushed me aside, trying to keep the phone pressed to his ear. But even as he tried to stay focused on Brady, I saw the huge smile that spread across his face.

I was so thrilled to hear him take charge with his manager, and I couldn't stop myself from dreaming about the summer we would have together. I could picture the trips to the theme parks and an afternoon on the beach. I would show him my favorite hike around a local lake. I was so absorbed in thoughts of the summer that I was surprised when Callum began saying his goodbyes to Brady.

"Sounds good. I'll talk to you in a month."

He hung up abruptly, without further niceties and, as soon as the phone was off, I let out the excited squeal I had been holding inside.

"That was amazing!" I cried. I wrapped my arms around Callum and hugged him close to me. He seemed a bit stiff, as if he might be shocked by what he had just done. But then he was hugging me back, and I felt him squeeze me close as relief flooded through his body.

"I can't believe I did that," he breathed out.

I pulled back so I could look at him.

"How did it feel?"

He thought about this for a moment, and then that smile spread across his face once more.

"It felt amazing! And it felt like it was a long time coming."

He leaned in and kissed me as he set his phone back onto the blanket.

"A whole month without band stuff?" I asked. I thought about the month stretched out before us. Would this turn into a month spent together, planning out the recording studio and going on silly first dates? I certainly hoped so.

"A whole month," he repeated. "Just the two of us."

I felt my stomach flip as he said this. For the first time in our relationship, we were on the same page. I leaned in and kissed him and Callum kissed me back. His hand came to my upper arm, and he squeezed it gently. I felt his happiness and commitment in that kiss. It was like Callum could finally breathe again, and now that all that business with the band was settled, we could block out the world for a moment.

Callum deepened the kiss, and I forgot we were outside in an open field where anyone could see us. I only knew Callum's lips on my own and the thrill of potential that coursed through both of us following our commitment to each other. Callum pressed forward so I was lying on my back, and I felt the rough flannel of the picnic blanket below us. He leaned over and kissed my neck and then his hand was on my stomach, his fingers drifting down to the hem of my shirt.

I smiled at him as he ran his fingers against the sensitive skin of my stomach and tried not to squirm as his fingers tickled me. He looked down at me with a smirk, enjoying this, and I grabbed his hand and pulled it to my chest, hugging his arm to me and bringing his body closer. He gazed into my eyes and then he dropped his lips onto mine. I felt the soft touch of them as he gently kissed me. The sweep of his tongue along my bottom lip sent a shiver through me.

Callum seemed to notice, because he instantly doubled down on our kissing. His arm was squeezed between our bodies as my breath came more quickly with each caress. I felt desperate for him, eager to hold every part of him against me and never let him go. Callum's leg hitched around my own, so I felt the comforting pressure of his hip pressed against mine as he rested on his elbow so he wouldn't crush me with his larger frame.

The hand between us was back to the peek of skin along my stomach, but now he ran his fingers up and under my shirt, above my belly button and toward my breasts. My whole body was buzzing, and even this gentle touch was electricity I could feel in every extremity. A gentle throbbing was building between my legs as Callum's hand found my breast and he rubbed against the hard nub of my nipple.

I gasped when he touched me, and Callum nipped gently along my jaw line as his fingers teased. A small moan escaped me, and the sound was enough to bring my head back to reality. I was reminded that we were outside in a public park where anyone could see us. This portion of the park was definitely more secluded, far away from the play-grounds and the dog park, and the sky was darkening around us, but we never knew who might come walking by.

"What if someone sees us?" I whispered, but I knew my voice was already betraying me. It was dripping with desire and an unspoken pleading for Callum to continue.

"Don't worry," he said. His hand switched to my other breast as he kissed me sweetly on the temple. "I'm watching. I'll stop if someone's coming."

Before I could protest, his hand snaked down to my waistband and he undid the button of my jeans. I pushed my hips up, trying to press against his leg that was still wrapped around my own, but he had positioned himself tight against my side so he could have better access to what was waiting between my legs. Still, I felt his arousal long and hard against my hip, and it brought waves of pleasure directly to my core.

Callum didn't wait to press below my underwear, and I gasped as he quickly dipped into my folds and felt the wetness waiting for him. I felt like a live wire as his touch made my hips jerk up in surprise, and then he was stroking me—long and insistent touches that brought quiet gasps as I felt pressure instantly building between my legs.

"Look at you," he whispered. My eyes were squeezed tight, but I blinked them open to look up at him. He continued his rhythm, growing faster with each stroke, and I could hardly keep my gaze on him for all the pleasure clouding my brain. He bent down and locked his lips with my own before locking his fingers over my sensitive button. I gasped and lifted my hips again, feeling how close I was and delighting in the way this man could make me melt beneath his fingers.

"I always knew it was you," he whispered. I thought about our first time together this summer: Our fast and surprising coupling in his theater dressing room. I thought about dinner and conversation at my house, and that day we toured the town looking at properties. And there was that beautiful moment earlier today when Callum played me his music in the middle of the hardware store. He had written a song about me and this summer.

But now I knew it wasn't the first time Callum had written a song on my account. All those years ago, in this very field, Callum had professed his love. And I was finally here to hear it.

Callum kissed me as his fingers moved fast between my legs. I pressed my lips against him as pressure built, and I let myself move toward it. I pushed my hips up and angled myself in the perfect position to feel his expert hands, his mouth on mine, and the warmth of his body beside me. I was close; another moment and I knew I would crash into pleasure that would ripple through me. I wanted to tell him not to stop, to keep going and do exactly what he was doing, but the words that came out of me were different.

"Stay with me," I gasped. And suddenly the pressure of his fingers brought me to completion. I cried out, much louder than I should have, and my whole body shook in the aftermath. Waves of pleasure washed through me, and Callum tucked my face into his neck as he held me, letting me ride out the journey. I squeezed my eyes closed and lost myself for a moment, content to disappear into the euphoria all around me, knowing that Callum was there to protect and keep me safe. We lay like that for a long moment, surrounded by the sound of cicadas emerging with the evening and feeling goosebumps rise on our skin as the air cooled around us.

"I'm not going anywhere," he whispered. I opened my eyes to see his adoring gaze looking down at me. Callum slid his fingers out from between my legs and I smirked at him, overwhelmed by what we had just done out in this field where things between us had begun.

"Me neither," I promised him.

EPILOGUE
CALLUM

"Sounds great, everyone. I think we got it!"

I spoke to the band from the control room where I was listening behind the audio engineers. The band in the booth looked back with smiles, amped up by the adrenaline of performing their own music in a professional recording studio. The group reminded me of the young musician I was when I first entered the industry.

"Great job," I said, slapping Aidan and Genevieve on the backs in a gesture of thanks. They had been my first hires for the recording studio, and I remembered how nervous I was as I interviewed them. But I was realizing that I should trust my instincts. These audio technicians had worked out wonderfully, proving themselves to be responsible and kind employees. A lot of the times they taught *me* things about the business!

The receptionist I had hired last month was also proving herself invaluable. Not only did Jess have a killer instinct for administration and calendars, she was already showing me how great of a marketer she was. Only a month in, and I was planning to move her from part-time receptionist to full-time executive assistant. After the success of my recent solo album, the recording studio was getting more inquiries than we could handle. I was going to need some more help to keep this place running.

A knock on the door drew my attention away from thoughts of our success. Instead, I smiled for an entirely new reason, knowing who would be waiting for me on the other side of the door.

"Look at that smile," Aidan teased. "If that's not a man in love, I don't know what is."

I rolled my eyes as Genevieve wagged her eyebrows at me. I ignored them as I crossed to the door and opened it to find Darcy standing there.

"Oh, good!" She said when she saw me. "I thought your 'recording' sign would never go off."

I slipped my arm around her back and pulled her close so I could kiss her. Darcy let out a small squeal of surprise as she shifted the picnic basket she held away from our bodies so it wouldn't get crushed.

"Hello to you, too," she said when I released her. "Are you ready for lunch?"

I smiled at her with a wide, goofy grin. It was strange to realize how happy it made me just to see her face. I couldn't get over the butterflies that flew around in my stomach anytime I knew we would be spending time together.

"I'm starving," I said as I grabbed her hand and walked with her back toward the main reception area.

"That's what happens when you work for six hours straight without a break!" Darcy laughed.

We had been into the studio early this morning since the band only had one day left of their visit in town. We'd completed their album, but there were a few songs I knew we hadn't quite unlocked yet, so I'd offered them an additional session this morning before their flights home. But it meant we didn't stop much throughout the day. Truth be told, my team and I were acquiring a bit of a reputation for getting absorbed in our work. Thankfully I had Darcy around to pull me out of these obsessive periods.

"I'm headed out for a bit," I told Jess as we crossed through the lobby. "Make sure you take a break too."

I saw Jess focusing on the computer screen in front of her, a new logo for the studio open in Photoshop.

"Yeah, I will," she mumbled, but I could tell she was barely listening. When Jess got like this, not much would pull her away from whatever was in front of her.

"Better yet, why don't you order food for the team? Aidan and Gen could use some fuel too."

The thought of free food actually made Jess look up at me, and she smiled.

"Sure thing, boss. Hey, Darcy, I didn't even see you come in!"

Darcy chuckled as she said hello to Jess who was already sorting through her drawers to find the takeout menus. With the staff taken care of, I opened the door to the old hardware store and held it open for Darcy to cross out in front of me.

"That place is really buzzing," she said, taking my hand again as we crossed the street to the park.

"I know," I answered. "It's hard to believe how far we've come in less than a year."

"How long do you have?" Darcy asked.

"About an hour. The guys are coming in to take another crack at that new song."

"The big *number one hit* the band keeps talking about?"

It had taken a bit of convincing, not to mention the hiring of a new manager, to get my bandmates to agree to my solo album. Despite some bruised egos, everyone seemed to realize it was what I needed to keep my creative juices flowing. Or at least they pretended to understand once I promised them we could do another the Horizon album by the end of the year. Lucky for us, the solo album had only increased the public's interest in our music.

"I know we're dangerously close to going off schedule," I said, "but we want the album to be perfect."

"Hey it's your studio," Darcy laughed. "I think you're entitled to a little extra recording time."

I looked up to see Liz, Maggie, and Alan waving enthusiastically from the park.

"I didn't know it was a family affair!" I laughed as Darcy pulled me across to Liz and her children. I pulled Maggie into a hug and ruffled Alan's hair as they told me all about the end-of-year concert they would sing at next week.

"I hope you didn't volunteer for this one," I said as I looked over at Liz. She looked back with a sheepish expression.

"How can you say no to these faces?" she asked as she put her hands on top of each child's head. "And I probably should have told you sooner, but ... I'm not the only one volunteering."

We settled down on to the picnic blanket Liz and the kids had set up while Darcy came across the street to get me.

"Let me guess," I laughed. "I'm running sound."

"Well, if you insist!" Liz laughed, and though I rolled my eyes at her, I was secretly excited to help my niece and nephew with their school play.

"You know, I have some people who might be even better suited for the job," I said, thinking about Aidan and Gen working hard back at the studio. Hopefully my employees had agreed on a lunch spot by now so they could order.

"As long as the parents and grandparents can hear their children, I don't care how it gets done," she said.

As we sat down for lunch, I was delighted by how ordinary it all felt. I never imagined I could meet my family in the park for lunch before I headed inside for my own afternoon session in the studio. I marveled at the way Liz and Darcy could weave in and out of conversations about work while still engaging the children in tidbits of information or questions about their days. And most of all, I delighted in how close Darcy sat to me, as if it were the most comfortable and ordinary thing for us to lean against one another as we snacked on cheese and fruit.

After they had satisfied their hunger, Maggie and Alan ran off toward the playground with Maggie squealing as Alan chased her. We laughed as we watched them.

"How did things go with that couple today?" Liz asked, turning her attention to Darcy. "Sorry I couldn't get out there to meet them."

"No problem," Darcy said. "Though if I had known how much work two offices was going to be, I might have reconsidered! I started a business with my best friend so we would actually see each other!"

"Which is why we need to hire more staff!" Ever since Darcy and Liz opened the second office, they had been debating about whether to bring in additional agents or some administrative assistant to help them with all the paperwork they were drowning in. I tried to stay out of the conversation whenever possible, since I had learned that getting myself in the middle of my sister and my girlfriend was an unenviable position to be in.

"We were talking about the couple I met with," Darcy said, guiding the conversation back to Liz's original question. "They're eager to buy, and no house of their own to sell since they're currently renting. I had barely asked the most basic information when she was suddenly telling me about their newborn and wanting to have a home for him to grow up in."

"How sweet!" Liz said.

"Adorable," Darcy agreed. Her hand rested casually on my knee and I brought my hand up to rest between her shoulder blades, simply happy to touch her and show her I was here for her.

A scream from the playground pulled our attention and Liz was instantly on her feet, motherly instincts kicking in.

"Alan!" She cried out. "Leave your sister alone!"

Liz set off toward the playground, continuing to scold Alan as she went. I felt Darcy's shoulders move as she laughed. She looked over and smiled, and then she leaned into me, allowing my arm to wrap around her in an embrace.

"Thanks for coming to lunch," she said as she tucked her head into the crook of my neck.

"Thank *you*!" I said. "If you hadn't pulled me out of that dark studio I would still be in there with headphones over my ears listening to the same two measures repeatedly."

"Well, good. I'm glad you're happy to be out here. I was starting to worry I was pulling you away from your work."

I pulled back then, and Darcy sat up to look at me. I wanted her to see how serious I was when I spoke.

"Darcy, the only thing that makes the work in the studio worthwhile is *you*. It's us. I'm doing all of this for us. And if I don't get these breaks out in the sun surrounded by people I love, then I can't create the art that I do. It's a recipe, and right now, I'd call this the secret ingredient."

She leaned in and kissed me before resuming her place leaning against my side.

"I love you," she said. It was so easy and matter of fact, you would have thought she had said it a hundred times before. And though it was the first time she had said this to me, the words did not surprise me at all. I was only surprised that I hadn't said them first.

"I love you," I responded. We sat in silence for a moment, watching Liz try to coax Maggie down from the top of the monkey bars. I thought about where we were a year ago and everything we had accomplished in the time since. And I thought about the years ahead of us and the adventures that were still in store.

"That couple looking for a house," I started, surprising myself with the words. "It has me thinking ... maybe it's time to think about getting our own place. If you're interested."

"Really?" Darcy asked. She looked at me with curiosity, and I could sense her excitement already growing. "Are you up for that?"

"Of course," I told her. "In case you haven't noticed by now, I'm not going anywhere. You're stuck with me."

"Promise?" Darcy laughed. I took her hand in my own and squeezed it tight in response.

"Alright," she continued. "So, we'll look for a house."

"Good," I smiled. My whole body felt warm at the idea of our future. And talking about it with Darcy was even better than dreaming about it. I looked over at her and smirked.

"Hmmm ... Now if only we knew a real estate agent ..."

Darcy pushed her shoulder into mine in a playful shove. I allowed myself to be knocked over from the blow, and we were soon on the ground, laughing and playfully pushing each other like giddy children without a care in the world.

· · ·

THE END.

If you enjoyed Second Chance at Us then you will love Beneath his Protection.

(Access Beneath his Protection by clicking here)

Sexy secret billionaire, club owner finds himself irresistibly drawn to the new girl in town in this scorching small-town romance. Brace yourself for a thrilling journey with twists and turns that will leave you breathless with anticipation. Get stuck in with chapter one on the next page!

SNEAK PEEK

BENEATH HIS PROTECTION

Who's the mysterious blue-eyed billionaire that owns the club downtown?

Kayla

I freeze as porcelain shards scatter across the coffee shop floor.
My heart races at the sight of the mesmerizing man before me.
He's *stunning*.

His aura of mystery and strength draws me in.
Igniting a fiery attraction I haven't felt in ages.
Something I wasn't prepared for after what happened with my ex.

Logan

Kayla's sass and beauty captivate me.
Though uncertainty lurks in her past.

As her ex resurfaces, I vow to shield her.
Even if it means revealing my secrets.

But keeping her safe means keeping my distance.
A struggle testing my resolve.
All I want to do is...

Touch her.
Hold her.
Do naughty things to her...

As we find solace on my secluded island paradise.
The reality back home remains ever-present.
Reminding us that our idyllic refuge is only temporary.

We must return and confront her ex.
But the dread of our love bubble bursting gnaws at me.
Casting a shadow over our uncertain future.

(Access Beneath his Protection by clicking here)

Chapter One
Kayla

I've heard many coffee mugs shatter while on shift in the Double Shot Café.

Never once had a mug shattered my world like this one.

It hit the floor, porcelain shards exploding over the fake tile. I clapped a hand to my mouth.

"I'm so sorry! I'll get this—" I started.

The words died in my throat as I glanced up to see the prettiest set of blue eyes I'd ever seen on a man. He blinked down at me holding my tray of spilled coffee. I was captivated.

Normally, I would crouch to pick up the broken pieces and shoo the customer away. It was our policy not to get shards stuck in customer's shoes, of course, and the last thing I wanted was to cause a scene. I already brought enough attention to myself daily with my comedic server's performance.

But this time, I did no such thing. I gazed into those icy blue eyes, entranced by the intelligence I saw swimming in them. They shifted as they analyzed me, questioning my intentions, glancing over my build, and reading my body language in the space of a second. I couldn't help but stare. How could anyone look away when a beautiful stranger happened to bump into them in the path of life—literally? It was a rare stroke of luck, something I thought had run dry in my life long before that day.

"My apologies," the man said.

A tingle went down my spine. His voice was the perfect balance of eloquent smoothness and authoritative baritone. It seemed fitting, coming from his five-foot, ten-inch frame of lean muscle. He wasn't a muscled guy, but he wasn't a runner, either—just like me. I wondered if I'd seen him at the gym. He looked familiar. There were only seven thousand people in Masonville, after all; I was bound to run into him if he was working out.

I realized he was waiting for me to say something, when he raised a brow. I shook myself from my trance, cleared my throat, and stood up straight.

"No need to apologize. I should know to watch where I'm going by now," I said.

"You can say that again!" Kennedy taunted from behind the bar. "How many mugs is that this month? Five?"

I rolled my eyes, ignoring my boss's remark. She always gave me crap about being a terrible server, but I practically ran the café for her, and she knew it. I turned back to the stunning specimen still standing only inches away from me.

"Would you mind stepping back so I can clean up?" I asked.

Before I've finished speaking, the man was holding up his hand to stop me.

"I'd rather me get cut than you."

He kneeled and scooped the large glass pieces into his hand. He tossed them in the trash can behind him, then brushed his hands off, shooting me a smile.

"There. Now, no one's hurt."

"I could have taken care of that, you know."

"I'm aware. You seem rather valuable to this café. Do you always tend to customers this fast?"

I snorted. "Who do you think I am, some teenager working a summer job?"

"No, I'd say you're quite the opposite. You have a great work ethic. I appreciated the personalized service."

When I say I never blush, I mean, I *never* blush. But in that moment, that man had me pink across the cheeks. I cursed myself for acting like a googly-eyed schoolgirl in front of this handsome hunk.

Then, in an instant, my embarrassment was put to an end by the sight of a cut on his finger. I immediately ran to the storage closet and grabbed the first aid kit.

"That was stupid of you, you know," I scolded him. "I could have swept up the glass with a broom."

The man shook his head, an amused smile playing on his lips. Good *Lord* was it attractive on him. I would have been sweating bullets in the space of three seconds had Kennedy not kept the air conditioning at a cool sixty-five.

"It's no big deal," he said.

"Well, I'm not about to get yelled at, so sit your butt down and let me patch you up," I ordered, pointing to a nearby chair.

The man's smirk only got more attractive as he shrugged his shoulders carelessly and sat down at the table. My heart hammered against my chest as I sat across from him, pulling out an antiseptic wipe and a small bandage. He didn't so much as wince when I wiped the blood away from his cut. Seriously, even I, with a high pain tolerance, couldn't stand the annoying sting of the antiseptic wipes on a cut. How tough did this guy think he was?

When I finished putting the bandage on his finger, he leaned back in his chair, giving me another once-over. I didn't miss the flash of interest in his eyes as he did so. It took all I had not to get up and slap him for checking me out in the middle of the café. Or maybe it didn't take any effort at all—he was *very* attractive himself, after all. His interest had my blood pumping faster than I cared to admit.

"Happy now?" he asked.

"Yes. Now Kennedy won't be all over my case the rest of the day."

"Good. I wouldn't want the best barista in town to have a bad day because of me."

His smirk transformed into a genuine smile. The kindness that had been hidden in those dreamy blue eyes suddenly came out into the open, lighting up his whole face. My lips parted in shock. Was it possible for him to be *more* attractive?

"You haven't made me have a bad day," I said, averting my eyes. "You just made it interesting, that's all."

"Well, I'm glad I could make it interesting."

He pulled his wallet out of his pocket and slid a bill

under his meal ticket. Then, he stood, adjusting his suit jacket over his shoulders as he did. I couldn't take my eyes off him. I felt like I was staring at a model.

"Oh, one thing before I go," he said. "What was your name?"

"It's Kayla," I said, "Kayla Thornston. And you are?"

"Logan Bauer. Pleasure to meet you."

He flashed me another stunning, overwhelmingly kind smile, then walked out the door, leaving me speechless. Logan Bauer...that name sounded familiar. I knew it from somewhere. Where had I heard it before?

My eyes flew wide when I realized the truth. Logan Bauer was the owner of the only night club in town, The Owl's Den. He was known for his tall, dark, and mysterious vibes. He hadn't lived here long, only moving to the town a handful of years prior. He started his night club right away, and the whole town flocked to it, finding the food and drink to be outstanding, and the staff incredibly personable.

Logan had been the talk of the town for a while. The rumor mill churned out story after story of his possible past, his reasons for starting a night club in the middle of nowhere, his potential relationship troubles, etcetera, etcetera. The stories spread like wildfire, but with time, they'd died down. I never knew that the mystery of the town was such a handsome, courteous man, with the most intriguing personality I'd ever encountered.

I looked under the ticket, only to clap a hand to my mouth. Logan had paid for his meal with a *fifty-dollar bill*. He'd only ordered a plain black coffee and a sesame bagel, totaling less than five dollars. The rest was a tip for me.

I went beet red in an instant. I ran to the bathroom to splash cold water on my face, cursing myself for letting him get to me so easily. Was this Logan's way of flirting? He certainly let on that he was interested, based on those tiny blue flames in his eyes as he very obviously checked me out. It's not like he had tried to hide it.

But I also wasn't about to deny my interest in him, either. He was the tall, blonde-haired, blue-eyed athlete of my dreams. He had my temperature up about ten degrees. I was not a woman to be swept off my feet, but man, did he tick all the boxes. There was no such thing as love at first sight...but there was something to be said about that initial spark of attraction, and from the most chance of circumstances.

Who knew I'd drop a mug and meet the most interesting guy in Masonville? I thought.

"Kayla! I need you out here!" Kennedy called.

"Coming!"

I dried my face, then ran back out to the bar to make the orders. I had all four espresso machines going at once, and I was doling out latte milk foams at the speed of light. Our rush hour had hit. Normally, I enjoyed the opportunity to throw myself into the work and forget about the rest of my life. It was a perfect time to shut off my brain and enjoy the smell of coffee and the sound of pleasant conversations in the background.

Not today, though. My mind was *full* of Logan Bauer. I saw his smile in my mind's eye, heard his baritone, smooth-as-honey voice, and felt the warmth of his hand in my own. I didn't mess up my coffee orders, but my mind was far from this café. It was with Logan, wherever he'd gone for the day.

When the morning rush finally died down, I took the chance to make myself a cappuccino. Kennedy joined me by the steamer as she wiped down the bar.

"What are you thinking about?" she asked.

I nearly dropped my cup. *"What?"*

"Kayla, don't play dumb with me. I see that glassy look in your eyes. Who's got your attention this time?"

I smiled sheepishly. "That guy from earlier."

"So, Logan's your type, is he?"

"Kennedy!" I gasped, frantically glancing around the café. Thankfully, it didn't seem like anyone heard her. "Don't go telling the whole world, please!"

"Oh, get over yourself. This isn't some high school romance. You're a grown-ass woman. If you like someone, say it loud and proud. Go pursue him if he's such a hottie."

"But I don't know anything about him," I said, looking at my reflection in the metal of the espresso machine. "What if he doesn't like brown-eyed brunettes? What if he's attracted to bodybuilders? I was only a runner all my life."

"Kayla, if you sit here asking yourself 'what if?' all day, the chance is going to pass you by before you ever decide to take it," she said, rolling her eyes. "Besides, if he's that picky, then he's not worth your time. He'd be stupid to miss out on an eleven like you."

My eyes nearly popped out of my head. "*Kennedy!*"

She only laughed to herself and went back to cleaning the bar.

I took a sip of my cappuccino, then bit my lip, considering her words. I didn't know anything about Logan, but the only way to figure him out was to talk to him. Maybe I *should* pursue him. It couldn't hurt to try, right?

(Access Beneath his Protection by clicking here)

Made in United States
North Haven, CT
26 August 2024

56579598R10138